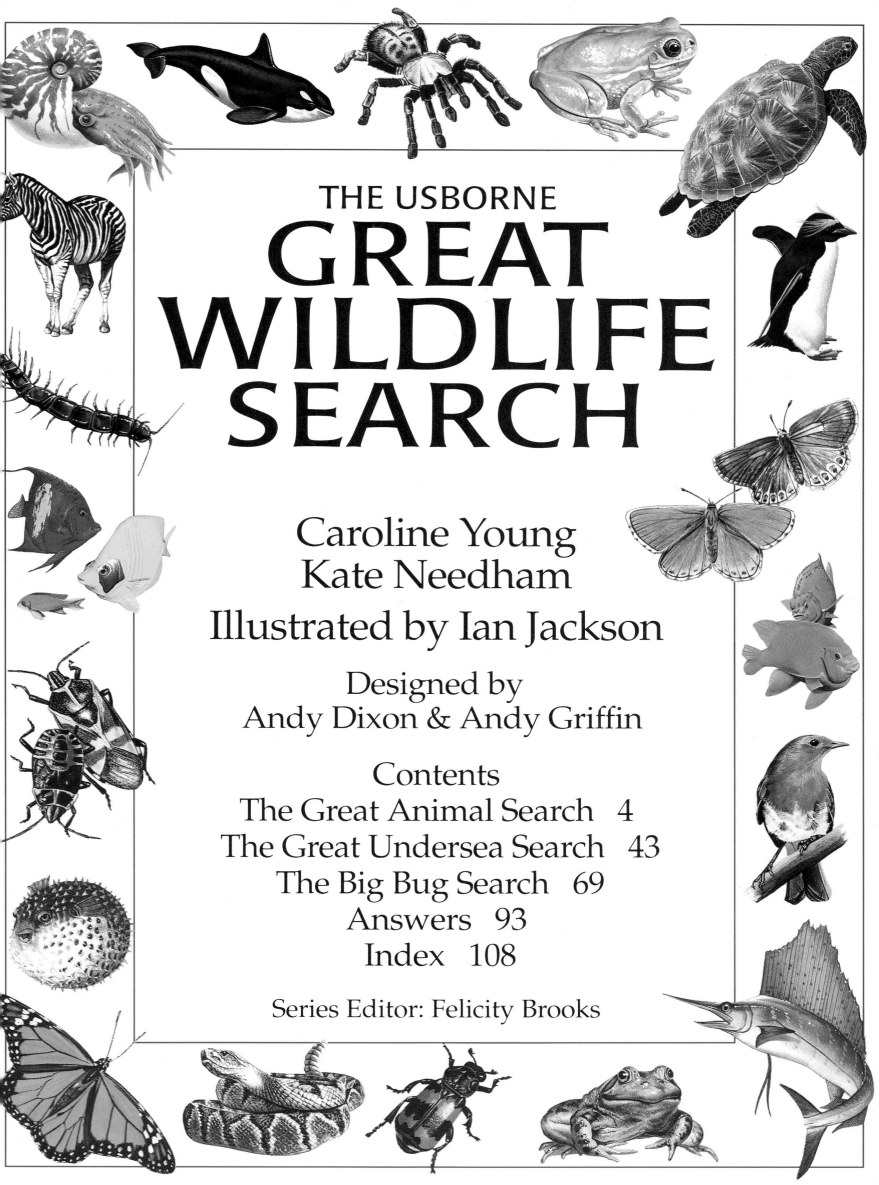

THE USBORNE
GREAT WILDLIFE SEARCH

Caroline Young
Kate Needham

Illustrated by Ian Jackson

Designed by
Andy Dixon & Andy Griffin

Contents

Series Editor: Felicity Brooks

Managing Designer:	Mary Cartwright
Design Assistant:	Susannah Owen
Editor (Big Bug Search):	Kamini Khanduri
Editorial Assistants:	Rosie Heywood
	Rachael Swann
Scientific Consultants:	Dr. John Bevan
	Dr. Davie Duthie
	Dr. John Rostron
	Dr. Margaret Rostron
Diving Consultant:	Reg Vallintine
Picture Researcher:	Sophy Tahta
Keys Illustrator:	Edwina Hannam

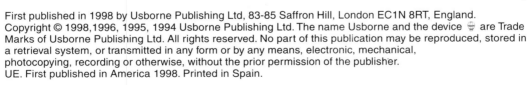

Contents

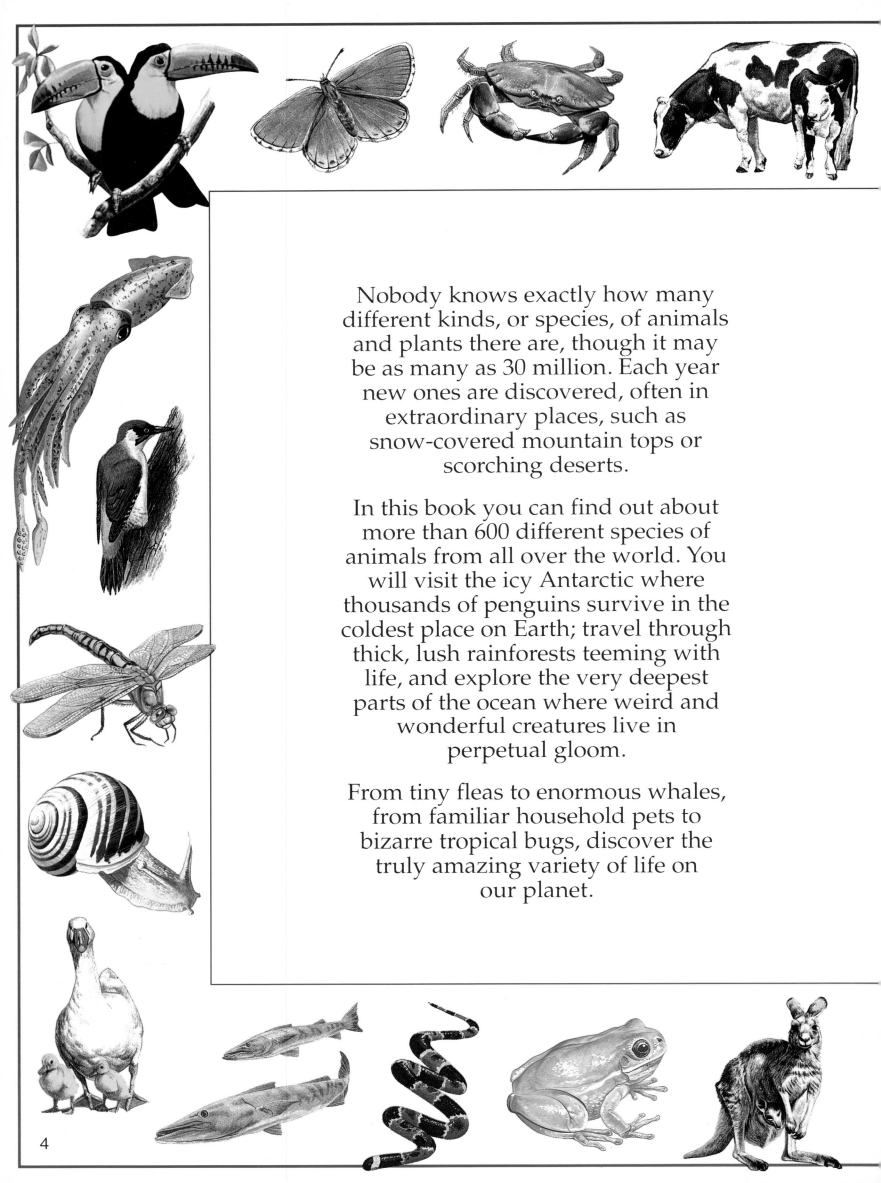

Nobody knows exactly how many different kinds, or species, of animals and plants there are, though it may be as many as 30 million. Each year new ones are discovered, often in extraordinary places, such as snow-covered mountain tops or scorching deserts.

In this book you can find out about more than 600 different species of animals from all over the world. You will visit the icy Antarctic where thousands of penguins survive in the coldest place on Earth; travel through thick, lush rainforests teeming with life, and explore the very deepest parts of the ocean where weird and wonderful creatures live in perpetual gloom.

From tiny fleas to enormous whales, from familiar household pets to bizarre tropical bugs, discover the truly amazing variety of life on our planet.

This is not just a book about animals, it's also a puzzle book, with thousands of things to spot. This is how the puzzles work, plus a few tips to help you solve them.

There are hundreds of things to find in each big picture in the book. In real life, there would not be as many in the same place at the same time.

Around the outside of each big picture, there are lots of little ones. The blue writing tells you how many of that thing you can find in the big picture.

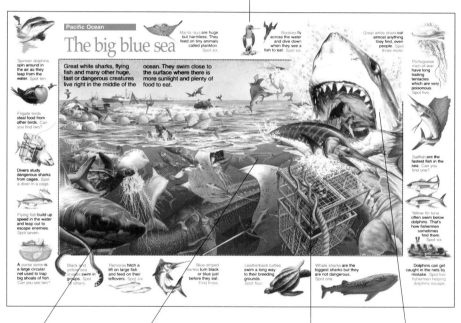

Pacific Ocean

The big blue sea

Great white sharks, flying fish and many other huge, fast or dangerous creatures live right in the middle of the ocean. They swim close to the surface where there is more sunlight and plenty of food to eat.

You can only see part of this shark but it still counts.

This manta ray in the distance counts too.

You will need to count all these snakes carefully.

This shark coming out of the picture counts as a little picture too.

The puzzle is to find all the things in the main picture. Some are easy, but others are tiny or partly hidden. Some animals look quite similar, so you will need to look very carefully to spot the difference. If you get stuck, you can look up the answers on pages 94 -107.

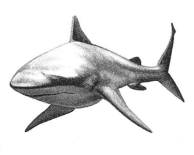

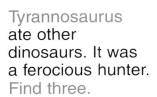

Tyrannosaurus ate other dinosaurs. It was a ferocious hunter. Find three.

Pteranodon flew on big wings of stretched-out skin. Find two others here.

Parasaurolophus had a curved, bony tube on its head. Can you spot three?

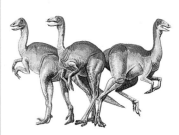

Struthiomimus looked a bit like an ostrich without feathers. Spot seven.

Back in time

Alamosaurus lived on marshy land, munching plants. Find two.

Seventy million years ago, part of North America probably looked like this. Animals called dinosaurs lived here. There are 51 creatures for you to find in this picture. Can you spot them all?

Pachycephalosaurus had a bony lump on its head for head-butting enemies. Can you find three?

Maiasauras laid their eggs in nests. Find one Maiasaura.

Deinosuchus' name means "terrible crocodile". Spot two.

Styracosaurus had a bony collar around its neck. Find one.

Ankylosaurus swung its bony tail like a club. Find two.

Quetzalcoatlus was a pterosaur, or "flying lizard". It was as big as a small plane. Spot two.

Stegosaurus had bony plates along its back to protect it from enemies. Find two.

Panoplosaurus was covered with knobs and spikes. Find five.

Anatosaurus had a kind of beak instead of a mouth. Spot three.

Corythosaurus had a hollow, bony plate on its head. Spot four.

Triceratops looked fierce, but it spent its time eating. Find two.

Dromaeosaurus stabbed its enemies with its sharp claws. Spot six.

Conifer forests

Skunks spray smelly liquid at their enemies. Find three.

Black bears are good at climbing trees. Even the cubs can do it. Find four bears.

Snowshoe hares have furry feet to run in the deep snow in winter. Spot six hares.

Lynxes' beautiful coats blend with the shadows. Can you find three lynxes?

Spruce grouse only eat leaves and buds from spruce trees. Can you find four grouse?

Wolverines are also known as "gluttons". This means greedy people. Find three.

Forests cover the top of North America and Canada. The trees in them are mainly conifer trees that keep their leaves all year. Not many people live there, but lots of animals do. Can you spot 80 animals in this picture?

North American martens are fast and fierce hunters. Find three martens.

Chipmunks eat all summer, and sleep all winter. Find eight.

Northern shrikes spend all day feeding their babies. Find two.

8

Long-eared owls have two feathery tufts on their heads. Find four.

Beavers can cut down trees with their sharp teeth. Spot eight beavers.

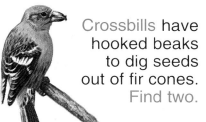

Crossbills have hooked beaks to dig seeds out of fir cones. Find two.

Moose can wade through water with their long, thin legs. Find six moose.

Fishers attack porcupines. They bite their soft tummies. Spot four fishers.

Brown bears teach their cubs what to eat. Find two and a cub.

Flying squirrels can glide between trees. Spot five squirrels.

Pumas are also called mountain lions or cougars. Spot three.

Ospreys swoop into water to catch fish. Find three.

Porcupines are covered in spikes called quills. Spot three.

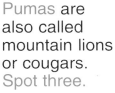

Mink slink along, looking for voles and insects to eat. Can you find three mink?

9

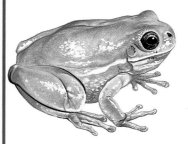

Green tree frogs have suckers on their feet to climb slimy branches. Find eight frogs.

Otters can even eat fish while swimming on their backs. Spot six.

Snail kites only like eating one kind of snail. Can you find two snail kites?

Zebra butterfly. Spot four.

Fisher spiders eat insects clinging to the bottom of plant stems. Spot one.

Steamy swamps

Alligators Spot six.

Swamps are so wet you can't tell what is land and what is water. Many animals live in these watery worlds.

This picture shows part of a swamp in Florida, in the US, called the Everglades. Can you find 85 animals here?

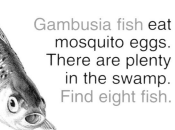

Gallinules are shy. They hide from enemies in the grass. Find four gallinules.

Gambusia fish eat mosquito eggs. There are plenty in the swamp. Find eight fish.

Bullfrog. Find three.

Bald eagles scoop fish up with their sharp claws. Find two.

Terrapins stick their skinny necks above water to take a look. Find ten.

Little blue herons wait for ages before spearing a fish. Spot two.

Raccoons use their front paws to scoop up fish and frogs from the water. Find six.

Cottonmouth snakes wiggle their bodies to swim along. Spot five.

Orb web spiders spin webs to catch passing insects. Find one.

Snapping turtles are experts at snapping up fish. Can you spot four turtles?

Anhingas dive underwater and stab fish with their beaks. Spot three.

Manatees swim slowly along, munching plants. Spot four.

Pileated woodpeckers keep their babies hidden. Spot three.

Garpike can easily tear up food with their sharp teeth. Spot three.

11

Dusty deserts

Trapdoor spiders crouch in tunnels and grab insects. Spot two.

Life is hard in the scorching deserts of North America. One part of them is so hot that it's called Death Valley.

This picture shows part of the Sonoran Desert. If you look closely, you'll spot 95 animals that live in this dusty place.

Coyotes often howl to each other to keep in touch. Can you find six?

Desert tortoises hide under the sand all day to stay cool. Spot four.

Burrowing owls move into empty burrows rather than dig them. Spot six.

Tarantulas are poisonous, but only enough to kill an insect. Find six.

Loggerhead shrikes push lizards onto cactus spikes. Spot four shrikes.

Black-tailed jackrabbits hop across the hot sand. Spot six jackrabbits.

Gila monsters lick insects' footprints to find them. Find four.

Gambel's quails blend in well with the desert. Can you find two?

Kangaroo rats get all the water they need from grains. Find six kangaroo rats.

Crafty gila woodpeckers build nests inside cacti. Spot seven.

Rattlesnakes shake their tails to make a scary rattle. Find three rattlesnakes.

Elf owls often move into empty woodpeckers' nests. Find five.

American fringe-toed lizards dig in the sand with their noses and toes. Find eight.

Swallow-tailed butterfly. Find six.

Roadrunners run in zig-zags, to confuse enemies. Spot three more.

Kit foxes, or swift foxes, run very swiftly across the sand. Find three foxes.

Chuckwallas hide between rocks. Enemies can't see them. Can you spot three?

Peccaries can even eat cacti with their tough teeth. Find ten peccaries.

Thick fur keeps polar bears warm. Spot three and two cubs.

The Arctic

Musk oxen don't mind snow. Their thick coats keep them warm. Can you spot nine?

In the Arctic, winter is so cold that the sea freezes. Many animals go to warmer places until spring. This picture shows the Arctic at the end of a long, cold winter. There are 101 animals here for you to spot.

Humpback whales like this one visit the Arctic. They "sing" as they swim.

Lemmings live in cosy tunnels under the snow all winter. Find 11.

Stoats even squeeze into lemmings' tunnels. Find three stoats.

Baby seals have pale fur which drops out after a few weeks. Spot four.

Ptarmigans are white in winter and brown in summer. Can you find five?

Arctic ground squirrel. Find three.

Snowy owls hunt during the long Arctic day. Find three.

14

Raven. Find three.

Narwhals have a horn sticking out above their mouths. Spot two narwhals.

Arctic foxes bury animals in the snow. It's like a freezer. Find five.

Wolves often hunt in a team called a pack. Spot ten.

Killer whales only kill fish and seals for food. Find two.

Walruses have plenty of fat to keep them warm. Find 12.

Caribou dig up plants under the snow. Spot 11 caribou.

Five kinds of seals live in the Arctic. Find one of each kind.

Harp seal

Ribbon seal

Ringed seal

Hooded seal

Bearded seal

White fur disguises Arctic hares very well. Find four others.

Beluga whale babies turn white when they are two. Find a mother and baby.

15

Under the sea

There are more than 20,000 kinds of fish in the world's rivers, lakes and seas. Some fish swim near the surface.

Others live in deep, dark water. This shows 22 kinds of sea creatures in the North Pacific Ocean.

Gulper eels can gulp down fish which are bigger than themselves. Find two eels.

These fishes' bodies light up in the gloomy deep water. Spot five of each kind.

Hatchet fish

Lantern fish

Fin whales swim along with their mouths open, swallowing food. Spot one.

Jellyfish sting small fish with their tentacles, then eat them. Find four jellyfish.

Angler fish wave a small fin above their mouths. Fish bite it and then get eaten. Find three.

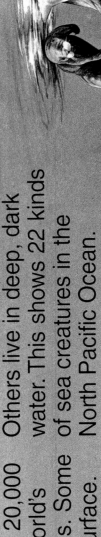

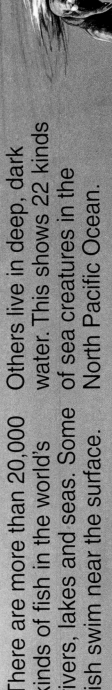

If an octopus is being chased, it squirts out cloudy brown ink. Can you spot two?

Sponge

Sea lily

Sea spider

It is cold and dark at the bottom of the sea. Spot three of each of these creatures there.

16

Fishermen catch marlin. Their sharp noses can be dangerous. Spot two.

Squid have ten arms with suckers on them to catch fish. Spot ten squid.

Huge basking sharks float near the surface of the sea. Can you spot one?

Dolphins often leap above the water. Nobody knows why. Spot four dolphins.

If skates are disturbed, they give enemies electric shocks. Find three.

Sea otters break open shells to eat the creatures inside. Find five otters.

Tuna

Herring

Sand eel

Giant squid have big eyes to help them see in deep water. Find two.

Dall's porpoises swim fast. You can see their spray from far away. Find five.

Beard-worms. Can you spot a group?

Groups of these fish swim near the surface. Spot a group of each.

17

Rainforests

Hoatzins are strange birds. They smell awful. Spot two and a baby.

Tapirs use their long noses to sniff for food among the bushes. Find three.

Emerald tree boas slither through the green trees. They are hard to spot. Find three.

Uakari monkey Spot six.

Sloths move very slowly. They can spend their whole lives in one tree. Spot three.

Humming-birds move their wings quickly and make a humming sound. Find three.

In rainforests, it rains almost every day. Trees and plants grow incredibly fast. This shows part of the Amazon Rainforest in Brazil. More kinds of animals and plants live here than anywhere else. Can you find 71 animals?

Toucans live in pairs. Their huge beaks are made of hollow bone. Spot four.

Black howler monkeys howl to each other to keep in touch. Spot four.

Silky anteaters look for ants. They lick them up with their long tongues. Find two.

Capybaras are good swimmers. They spend most of their time in the water. Spot ten.

Golden lion tamarins have manes of golden hair, like lions. Find three.

Golden cock-of-the-rock. Spot two.

Jaguars climb trees and swim across rivers to catch animals. Find one.

Anacondas can squeeze animals to death. Then they eat them whole. Find three.

Giant armadillos have thick, scaly skin to keep teeth and claws out. Spot two.

Amazon Indians use poison from arrow-poison frogs on the tips of their arrows. Find nine.

Blue and yellow macaw

Coral snakes are poisonous, so animals do not eat them. Spot three.

Spider monkeys are expert tree-climbers. Their tails help them hold on. Find three.

Many kinds of parrots live in the forest. Find one of each kind.

Hyacinth macaw

Golden conure

Scarlet macaw

Hot and dry

Camels can last a week without water. Spot eight adults and a baby.

Fennec foxes even hear insects moving with their huge ears. Find four foxes.

Toad-headed agamid lizard. Spot four.

Desert hedgehogs try and keep out of the sun. Find four hedgehogs.

Mauritanian toad. Spot one.

Desert hares sit in the shade during the heat of the day. Find four hares.

Coursers can run fast to escape from enemies. Find four coursers.

Deserts are the hottest, driest places on Earth. This picture shows part of the Sahara, the biggest desert in the world. You might be surprised by how many animals manage to live here. Can you find 124?

Sahara gecko. Spot one.

Jerboas hop across the sand like mini-kangaroos. Spot five.

Sand vipers bury themselves deep in the sand to stay cool. Find four vipers.

20

Desert centipede. Spot three.

Find one sandgrouse and her three chicks.

Darkling beetle. Spot three.

Skinks are hard to spot in the desert sand. Find four skinks.

Tiger beetles make a tasty snack for some desert animals. Spot three.

Little owl. Spot four.

Sand cats hunt smaller animals. Their fur blends in with the sand. Spot four cats.

Desert locusts. Find four.

Sidewinders slither along with an S-shaped wiggle. Find four sidewinders.

Scorpions sting animals with their poisonous tails. Spot three scorpions.

These animals don't mind the heat. They hardly need anything to drink.

Addax. Find five.

Dorcas gazelle. Spot eight.

Oryx. Spot ten.

Barbary sheep. Spot 20.

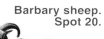

Lanner falcon. Find two.

Sand rat. Spot three.

21

African plains

Female elephants and babies live together. Male elephants live alone. Find seven.

Cheetahs run faster than any other animal, but they can't do it for long. Spot two.

Gerenuks can stand up on their back legs to reach the tastiest food. Spot two.

When vultures are flying, they can spot a meal a long way away. Spot nine vultures.

Ostriches are birds, but they can't fly. Find three ostriches and their nest.

Many of the world's best-known animals live in Africa, on huge, grassy plains. There are 17 kinds of animals here.

If you look closely, you can see what each kind eats. Most eat grass and leaves. Some kill other animals to eat.

Big groups of wildebeest wander across the plains, looking for food. Find eight.

If enemies attack rhinos, they charge at them, horn first. Spot three rhinos.

Baboon babies often ride on their parents' backs. Find eight baboons.

Hippos enjoy soaking in mud. It stops their skin from drying out. Find six.

Giraffes can reach food that no other animal can get to. Find four giraffes.

If a zebra sees an enemy, it barks, to warn the others. Spot eight zebras.

Warthogs snuffle along, digging up food with their long tusks. Spot three warthogs.

Wild dogs roam the plains, searching for something to eat. Spot eight.

Thomson's gazelles jump and flash their white bottoms to confuse enemies. Spot ten.

Leopards often drag their food up into a tree to eat it in peace. Find two leopards.

Male lions look fierce, but lionesses do the most hunting. Spot six lions.

Lioness

Lion

Kori bustards are the heaviest flying birds on Earth. Can you find two bustards here?

Spotted fallow deer are hard to see in the shadowy woods. Spot six deer.

Hidden homes

Moles tunnel underground. They are almost blind. Spot one.

Weasels often move into a home that another animal has left. Spot four weasels.

Woods like this are busy places in the spring. Many animals and birds are making homes for their babies.

There are 18 different kinds of animals in this wood. Can you spot where each kind makes their home?

Magpies make messy nests and a lot of noise. Can you spot two magpies here?

Dormice sleep all winter. When they wake up, they start building a home. Spot five.

Wild boar babies are hard to see in the long grass in the woods. Can you spot eight boars?

When a shrew family goes out, each shrew holds onto the one in front. Spot ten.

Jays bury acorns in winter. In spring, they dig them up to eat. Spot four.

Woodpeckers grip trees with their claws while they eat insects. Find four.

Several rabbit families live together in one home. Spot nine rabbits.

Badgers only come out when it is getting dark. Can you spot four badgers?

Nightjars sit still all day. Their feathers blend well with the woods. Spot two.

Squirrels build one home for winter and another for summer. Spot four squirrels.

Tawny owls fly silently. They can catch animals without being heard. Spot three.

Both fox parents look after, and teach, their cubs. Can you spot five foxes?

Horseshoe bats only start coming out of their homes as darkness falls. Spot ten.

Male
Female
Stag beetles. Spot two.

If hedgehogs are scared, they roll up into a tough, spiny ball. Spot four hedgehogs.

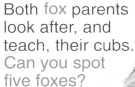

25

By the sea

Rotting seaweed is a tasty meal for sandhoppers. Can you spot some sandhoppers?

Most starfish have five arms. If one breaks off, they grow a new one. Spot five.

Redshank use their long, thin beaks to find worms in the mud. Spot three.

Hermit crabs live in empty shells. As they grow, they move into bigger ones. Find four.

Spiny sea urchins push themselves along with their tough spikes. Spot three.

Many people visit beaches, but do they know that thousands of animals live under the sand, in pools of seawater or on the cliffs?

The sea covers this beach, and goes out again, twice every day. When it is out, the beach looks like this. Can you spot 145 animals?

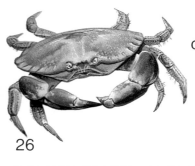

Crabs use their big claws to catch food. They can walk sideways, too. Spot six.

Puffin

Kittiwake

Razorbill

Guillemot

Many birds build their nests on the cliffs. Can you spot ten of each of these kinds?

Acorn barnacles grow hard coats around themselves. Can you find some here?

Lobsters are shy, but can give a nasty pinch with their big front claws. Spot two.

Cormorants stand with their wings open to dry their feathers. Find three.

A snakelocks anemone simply splits in half to make two anemones. Find ten here.

Prawns use their long feelers to search for tiny creatures to eat. Find ten prawns.

On land, beadlet anemones look like blobs. In water, they look like this. Spot five.

Many seashore animals live in hard shells. Spot ten of each of these four kinds.

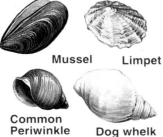

Mussel   **Limpet**

Common Periwinkle   **Dog whelk**

Blennies hide in wet places while the sea is out. Spot six.

Oystercatchers knock shellfish off rocks with their sharp beaks. Can you spot six?

27

Mountains

Bar-headed geese fly over the Himalayas each year. Can you spot ten geese?

Snow leopards, or ounces, hunt at night. They are harder to spot then. Find four.

Himalayan ibexes can clamber up slippery slopes to find food. Spot ten ibexes.

You can probably smell a takin before you see it. They smell oily. Spot two.

Male markhors spend the summer away from the females. Spot three males.

Life is not easy high up in the mountains. It's cold and windy, and the ground is often covered with snow.

The 83 animals here live in the Himalayas, the highest mountains in the world. Can you spot them all?

Himalayan black bears live in forests on the mountain slopes. Find three.

Wallcreepers climb down slopes head first. Their claws help them grip. Spot four.

Apollo butterfly. Find three.

If an animal dies, Himalayan griffon vultures swoop down and eat it. Spot six vultures.

Pikas let plants dry in the sun, then store them to eat in winter. Find six pikas.

Lammergeiers fly above the mountains, looking for dead animals to eat. Spot three.

Yaks have a coat of short fur, with long, shaggy hair on top to keep warm. Find five.

Some people think a yeti, or "abominable snowman", made these footprints. Spot some.

Male tahrs have thick fur and a collar of long hair around their heads. Spot three.

While a group of bharals is eating, one keeps a look out for enemies. Spot two.

Alpine choughs push dead insects into cracks in rocks, to eat later. Spot ten choughs.

Marmots sleep in a burrow all winter. They block the door with grass to stay warm. Spot six.

Golden eagles are strong enough to carry off a baby deer. Spot two eagles.

Light and dark

Indian tailor-birds sew nests from leaves and grass. Spot three.

Tigers creep up behind animals. They leap on their backs and kill them. Find one.

Great Indian hornbills like this one use their big beaks to reach any hidden fruit.

Giant flying squirrels glide silently between the jungle trees. Can you spot one?

Gavials catch fish by sweeping their long jaws from side to side. Spot three.

Indian elephants often march through the jungle in a line. Find four elephants.

Thick, hot rainforests are often called jungles. The story 'Jungle Book' is set in a jungle like this one, in India. These pictures show the jungle by day and at night. Look at both of them and try to spot which of these animals come out during the day and which at night.

Peacock

Peahen

Male peacocks shake their tails to impress the female peahens. Find one of each.

If muntjac deer are scared, they make loud barking noises, like a dog. Find two.

Slender lorises even walk on thin twigs, like this. Find one.

 Leopards are expert tree-climbers and hunters. Find one leopard.

 Dholes are wild dogs. They whistle to each other to stay in touch. Can you find four?

 Pangolins curl up into a tight ball. Their scaly skin protects them. Find one.

 Lazy sloth bears eat insects, fruit and even flowers. Can you spot a sloth bear?

 Leopard cats look like mini-leopards. They are very shy. Can you spot one?

Madras tree shrews live hidden up in the trees, eating insects. Spot one.

Mongooses are brave. They even tease, and then kill, cobras. Spot one mongoose.

Gaurs are a kind of cow. If they are scared, they whistle. Spot two.

The poison from a king cobra's bite can kill a person in half an hour. Spot one.

Bonnet macaques get their name from the tufts of hair on their heads. Spot ten.

31

Magical world

Bottlenose dolphins often leap over waves, following boats. Spot six dolphins.

If giant clams sense any danger, their huge shells shut tight. Find two giant clams.

Sea squirts. Find six.

Parrot fish use their hard lips to bite off lumps of coral to eat. Spot two parrot fish.

Sea cucumber. Spot two.

Stone fish lie on the seabed, looking like stones. Can you spot two?

Barracudas are fierce hunters, snapping up other fish. Spot three barracudas.

When tiny sea creatures called corals die, their skeletons are left in the sea. Over thousands of years, millions of these build up to make a reef. The biggest reef in the world is the Great Barrier Reef, near Australia. Can you spot 125 animals and fish here?

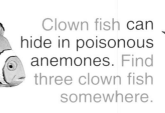

Clown fish can hide in poisonous anemones. Find three clown fish somewhere.

Wrasses go into other fishes' mouths and clean their teeth. Spot two.

Snapper

Red emperor

Blue and gold angelfish

Blue damselfish

Goldman's sweetlips

Spot which fish doesn't belong in each of these five groups.

Sea sponge.
Find three.

Dugongs use their big top lip to pull plants from the seabed.
Find three.

Sea horse babies grow in a pouch on their father's tummy. Spot six sea horses.

Lion fish.
Find two.

Wobbegong sharks often lie still on the seabed, looking like shaggy rugs.
Find one.

Bright flame shrimps nibble bugs off fishes' skins. Spot three shrimps.

Tiger cowrie.
Spot three.

Manta rays flap through the water with their mouths open, catching food. Find two.

Blue sea star.
Find two.

Can you guess how strange-looking hammerhead sharks got their name? Spot one.

There are many different kinds of coral. Can you find a clump of these four kinds?

Brain coral

Sea fan

Staghorn coral

Plate coral

Crown of thorns starfish eat coral. They can destroy whole reefs. Find four starfish.

Bright sea slugs slither across the coral. Spot three of each of these kinds of slug.

Naked sea slug

Spanish dancer

Saco-glossan sea slug

Kangaroos use their big back legs to jump high up into the air. Spot ten.

Few animals risk attacking a thorny devil. Its spiky skin is too tough. Spot four.

Marsupial moles are always digging. They rarely come above ground. Find three.

Quolls have long noses for sniffing out food, and sharp teeth to eat it with. Spot two.

Out and about

Shingle-backed skinks stick their blue tongues out at enemies. Spot two.

A lot of Australia is dry land, without many trees. People call it the outback. Not much rain falls, and it's very hot.

Finding enough to eat and drink is tricky. There are 75 animals somewhere in this picture. Can you spot them?

Dingos are wild dogs. They live and hunt in a big group. Can you find six dingos?

Kookaburras sound as if they are laughing when they call to each other. Spot four.

Water-holding frogs soak up water like sponges. Spot three.

Mallee fowl lay their eggs in piles of leaves, covered with sand. Find two birds.

Frilled lizards have a fold of skin like a collar around their necks. Spot three.

Bandicoots often dig. Their babies snuggle in a safe pouch under their tummies. Spot two.

Goannas prefer to run away from their enemies than fight them. Spot three.

If echidnas are scared, they bury themselves. Only their spines show then. Spot three.

Hairy-nosed wombats live in underground burrows. Find three wombats.

Budgerigars or parakeets often fly around in a big flock. Find 20 budgerigars here.

Hopping mice usually run, but they can also hop fast on their back legs. Spot two.

Emus are fast runners, but they cannot fly at all. Can you spot three emus?

35

Antarctica

Sperm whales can stay underwater for an hour before coming up for air. Find one.

Emperor penguin chicks snuggle between their parents' feet. Spot a chick and five adults.

Antarctica is the coldest place on Earth. The sea is frozen nearly all year. Icy winds blow across the land.

It's hard to survive here, yet millions of birds and seals do. There are 195 animals and birds for you to find here.

Weddell seals can stay under the freezing water for an hour. Find five.

Rockhopper penguins are good at hopping on snow and rocks. Find 80.

Crabeater seals don't eat crabs. They eat tiny sea animals called krill. Find four.

Blue whales are easily the biggest animals on Earth. Can you spot one here?

Wandering albatrosses glide over the sea on their huge wings. Find one.

Macaroni penguins have feathers called crests on their heads. Spot nine.

36

Blue-eyed shag. Spot three.

Gentoo penguins lay their eggs in nests made of stones. Spot 21 gentoo penguins.

Ross seals live on the solid ice away from other Antarctic animals. Find four.

Baby minke whales stay with their mothers for about a year. Spot a whale and her baby.

Chinstrap penguins sometimes lay their eggs on snow. Find 12 chinstraps.

Leopard seals catch penguins jumping into the sea. Spot five leopard seals.

Skuas fly over penguins' nests, waiting to kill their chicks. Find four skuas.

Adélie penguins leap from the sea onto the ice. Can you find 13?

Giant petrels eat so much they have to make themselves sick before taking off. Find four petrels.

King penguins lay one egg. Both parents guard it. Spot ten.

Male elephant seals fight to see who is stronger. Find ten elephant seals.

Fox

A closer look

Small white butterfly

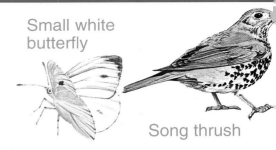

Song thrush

Tips

❁ Birds often come to a garden with a bird-table. They like eating cheese, seeds, fat and nuts.

❁ Lots of animals live in a pond. Others bathe in it, drink from it, or come to catch the animals in it.

❁ A "wild" patch of garden is a great place for insects to hide. Wild flowers might grow there, too.

❁ Berries on plants give birds a tasty meal. Plants that climb walls give them a nesting spot.

❁ Butterflies love bright flowers which smell beautiful. Try planting some in your garden.

❁ Flowerpots make a good home for some animals. Logs are handy for them to shelter under, too.

Animals don't only live in wild places. Lots live in gardens, like this one. There are 31 different kinds here. Can you find two of each? On this page, there are ideas for things which may make more animals visit your garden.

Robin

Small tortoiseshell butterfly

Bumblebee

Garden spider

Vole

Blackbird

Snail

Earthworm

Wren

Dragonfly

Wood mouse

Woodlouse

Newt

Magpie

Red admiral
butterfly

Hedgehog

Centipede

Greenfinch

Earwig

Frog

Slug

Chaffinch

Bullfinch

Peacock
butterfly

Toad

Wasp

Mole

Millipede

39

On the farm

Baby turkeys are called poults. Find three turkey poults.

Farmers keep cows for their milk. A cow's baby is called a calf. Can you spot a calf?

Farmers train sheepdogs to help them control their sheep. Find three sheepdog puppies.

Shetland ponies are small but they are hard workers. Find a Shetland foal.

Rats often steal other animals' food. Some farmers poison them. Spot three baby rats.

Farmers keep animals for their milk, meat, wool or eggs. Wild animals live on farms too. There are 19 kinds of animals in this picture. Each one has some babies hidden somewhere. Can you match the babies to the animals?

Farmers keep goats for their milk. Baby goats are called kids Spot two kids.

Crows eat crops, so farmers make scarecrows to scare them off. Find a baby crow.

Baby geese are called goslings. Feathers called down keep them warm. Find three.

Mice often build their nests in unusual places. Can you find four baby mice?

Cats catch mice and rats. Find three baby cats, or kittens.

Ducks swim on ponds. Find four baby ducks, or ducklings.

Bats sleep all day. Their babies eat at night. Spot two babies.

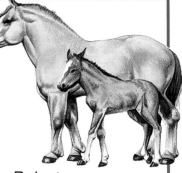

Baby horses are called foals. Shire horses work hard on farms. Find a shire foal.

Some chickens live inside, others roam outside. Can you spot three chicks?

Pigs roll in muck, but like clean straw to sleep on. Find four baby pigs, or piglets.

Many farmers keep donkeys to carry loads. Spot one baby donkey, or foal.

Rabbits live in underground burrows. Spot three baby rabbits.

Barn owls hunt at night, swooping on mice and rats. Spot two owl chicks.

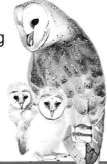

Baby sheep are called lambs. They are born in the spring. Find two lambs.

41

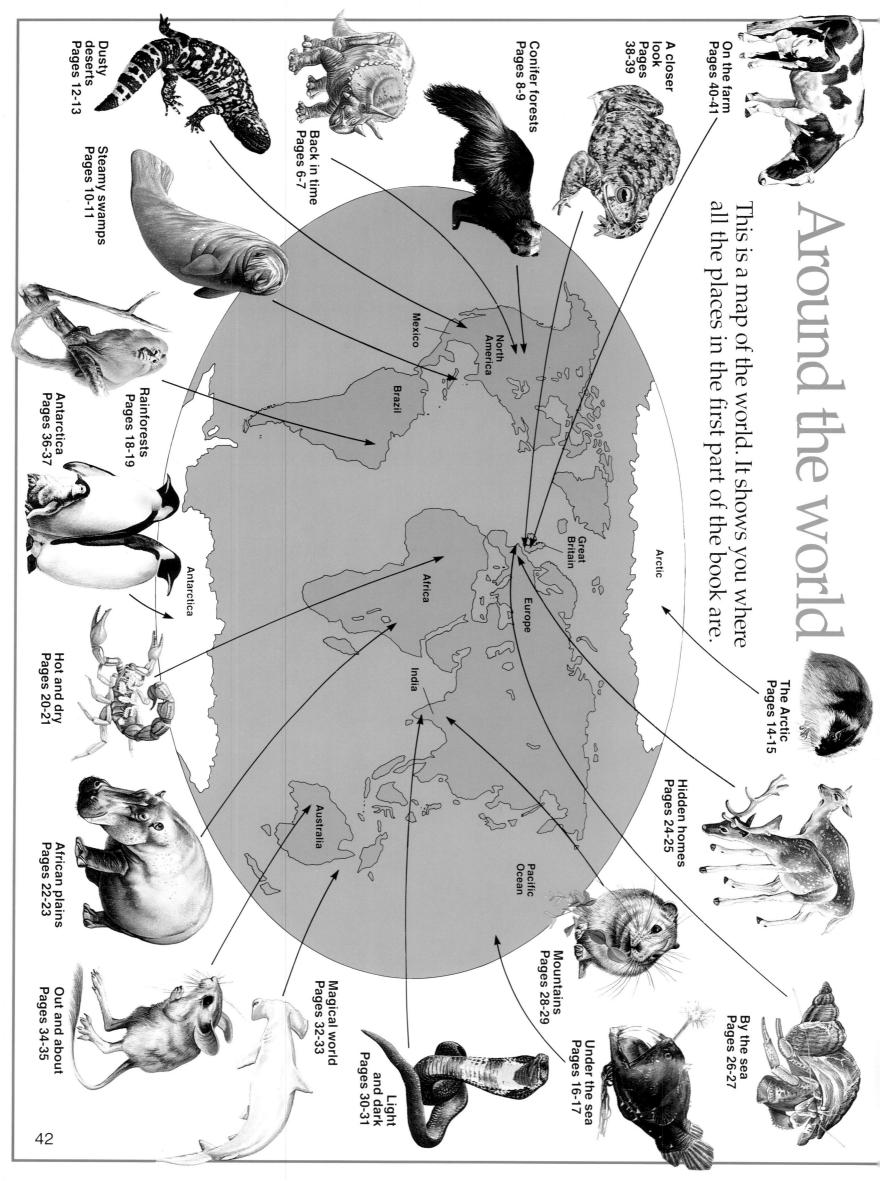

Around the world

This is a map of the world. It shows you where all the places in the first part of the book are.

Mexico

North
America

Brazil

Africa

Great
Britain

Europe

Arctic

India

Australia

Antarctica

Pacific
Ocean

The Great Undersea Search

The world's seas and oceans cover over two-thirds of our planet. They contain an astonishing variety of animals and plants, from the warm surface all the way down to ocean trenches over 6km (4 miles) below.

The second part of this book takes you on an exciting undersea safari. You will dive down to explore coral reefs, come face-to-face with some very strange creatures in the murky depths of the Atlantic, and look for pirate treasure in the Caribbean. On the way, you'll meet man-eating sharks, huge blue whales, poisonous jellyfish, giant octopuses and an incredible variety of fish.

Life on Earth began in the oceans over 500 million years ago. Turn the page to see some of the enormous and extraordinary creatures which swam in prehistoric seas.

Prehistoric seas

Placodus had a very strong jaw. Find two.

Ammonites used their tentacles to catch food. Find 13.

Two hundred million years ago, dinosaurs ruled the land and giant creatures swam in the seas. Smaller ones lived there too. Some are still around today. Look closely to find 21 different creatures in this scene.

Banjo fish were ancient relatives of skates and rays. Can you see four more?

Ichthyosaurus gave birth under water. Find two adults and three babies.

Jellyfish lived up to 600 million years ago. Can you see four?

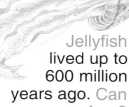

Giant sea turtles like archelon could hide inside their hard shells. Spot two.

Sea lilies are animals not flowers. Can you find a group of them?

Rabbit fish get their name from their funny faces. Find two.

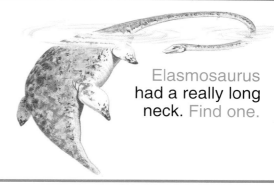

Elasmosaurus had a really long neck. Find one.

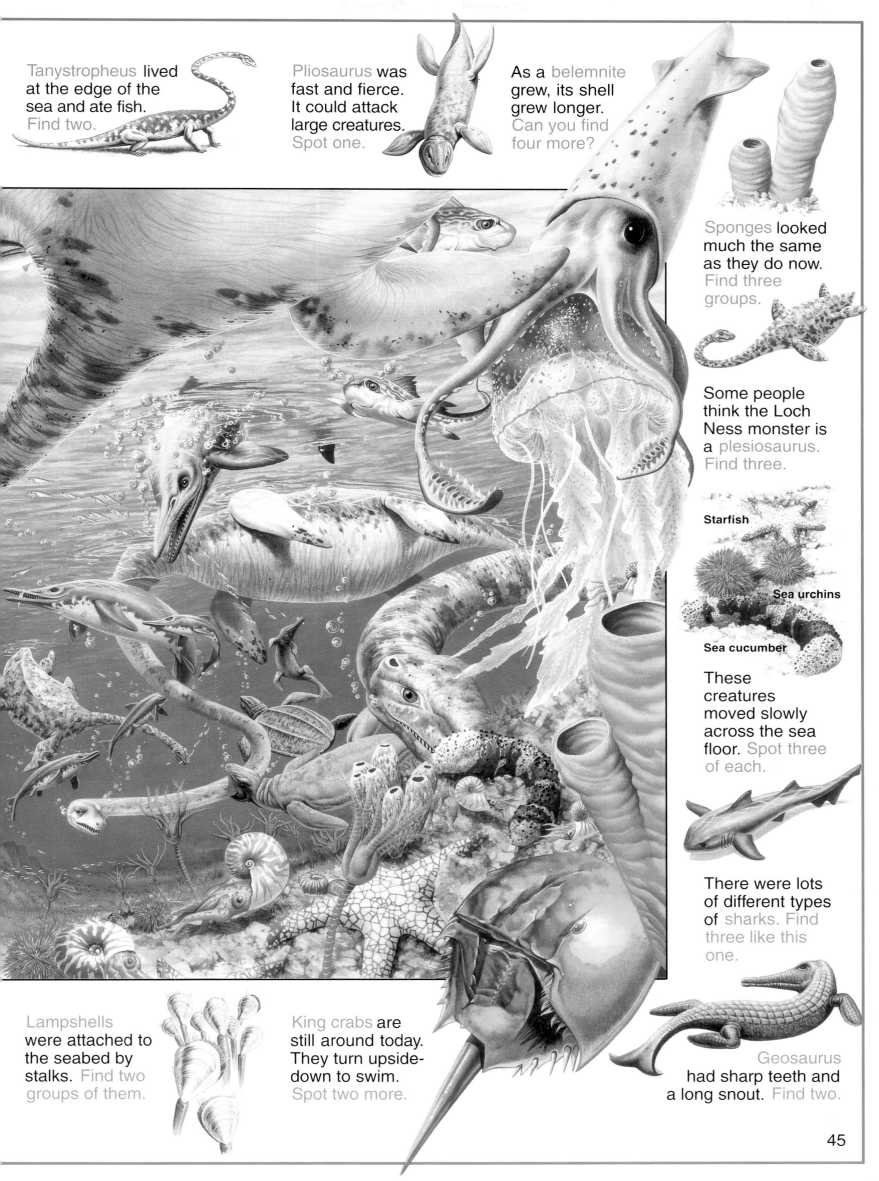

Tanystropheus lived at the edge of the sea and ate fish. Find two.

Pliosaurus was fast and fierce. It could attack large creatures. Spot one.

As a belemnite grew, its shell grew longer. Can you find four more?

Sponges looked much the same as they do now. Find three groups.

Some people think the Loch Ness monster is a plesiosaurus. Find three.

Starfish

Sea urchins

Sea cucumber

These creatures moved slowly across the sea floor. Spot three of each.

There were lots of different types of sharks. Find three like this one.

Lampshells were attached to the seabed by stalks. Find two groups of them.

King crabs are still around today. They turn upside-down to swim. Spot two more.

Geosaurus had sharp teeth and a long snout. Find two.

45

Shipwreck

Some wrecks have hidden treasure. There are 18 gold bars to find here.

All parts of a wreck are soon covered with coral. Can you find the anchor?

Reef sharks look dangerous but they rarely attack divers. Find three.

This ship was carrying bikes. Can you find three covered with coral?

Napoleon wrasses are large, friendly fish which often follow divers. Spot three.

With an eye and a nostril on each side of its wide head, a hammerhead shark sees and smells well. Find four more.

When you dive down to explore a wreck, you never know what you may find. There may be strange creatures lurking in the depths, or treasure buried in the sand. This ship sank years ago. Now it's covered in coral.

Crocodile fish have shiny green eyes. Spot one hiding on the sea bed.

Corals of all shades grow on the wreck. Spot four pink clumps.

Parrot fish nibble the corals with their beak-like mouths. Spot three.

This diver is going down to explore the wreck. Can you find seven more?

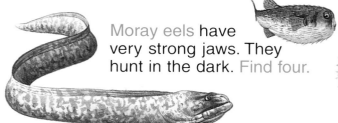
Moray eels have very strong jaws. They hunt in the dark. Find four.

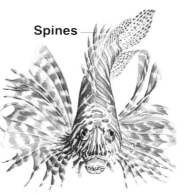
When they are scared, puffer fish blow up like spiky balloons. Can you see all four?

Spines

Lion fish have poisonous spines along their backs. Can you see two?

Cleaner fish clean the mouths and gills of larger fish. Spot four at work.

Blue spotted groupers like to live inside holes in the wreck. Find four.

These small fish recognize each other by their bright markings. Find 20 of each.

Angel fish

Butterfly fish

Anthias

Divers carry flashlights to see inside the darkest parts of a wreck. Spot four.

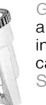
Glass fish swim around together in large groups called schools. Spot one school.

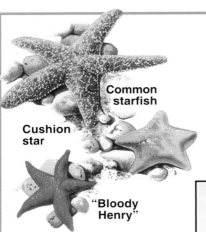

Common starfish

Cushion star

"Bloody Henry"

There are many types of starfish. Most have five arms. Spot four of each of these.

Beadlet anemones close up tightly to keep moist until the sea returns. Spot 20.

Hermit crabs live in empty shells. They move into a new house as they grow. Can you find two?

Limpets

Mussels

Some animals that live in shells cling to the rocks. Find five groups of each of these.

Rocky shore

Kittiwakes live on the cliffs and fish in the sea. Can you count 50?

The sea comes in and out twice each day on this rocky shore. When it goes out, many creatures are left behind in pools among the rocks like this one. If you look closely you will find over 100 creatures here.

Grey seals have large eyes to see in cloudy water and thick fur to keep them warm. Spot nine.

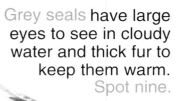

Butterfish are long and thin with spots along their backs. Find four more.

With eyes on top of their heads, rock gobies can spot danger above. Find two.

Octopuses can squeeze into tiny spaces. Can you find one?

Some rocks have fossils like these ammonites in them. Find ten.

Oystercatchers use their sharp beaks to eat shellfish. Spot three more.

Shore crab

Edible crab

Velvet swimming crab

Crabs can give a painful nip if you pick them up. Find three of each type.

Blennies use their fins to walk to a new pool. Spot three.

Acorn barnacles attach themselves to any hard surface. Find some on rocks, crabs and mussels.

Prawns are hard to spot as they are almost transparent. Find seven.

Can you see a net and bucket that someone has left behind?

Squat lobsters have huge front legs that are bigger than their bodies. Spot two.

Bows

Icy seas

When polar bears swim, a layer of fat and thick fur keeps them warm in the icy water. Spot four.

Research ships have especially strong bows to break through the ice. Spot one.

Beluga whales are called "sea canaries" because they sing to each other. Spot three.

Baby seals are called pups. They have fluffy white coats. Spot three.

Nautilus was the first submarine to cross the Arctic under the ice. Can you see it?

The Arctic Ocean is so cold that two-thirds of it is covered in ice all year round. Despite the freezing water, plenty of creatures live here. Scientists also visit to study the ice and learn about the world's changing climate.

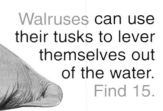

Walruses can use their tusks to lever themselves out of the water. Find 15.

Scientists attach transmitters to some animals to find out how they live. Spot one.

Bearded seals use their long curly whiskers to find shellfish. Find three.

50

Male narwhals have a long spiral tusk that is actually a huge front tooth. Find eight.

Arctic terns fly from the very north to the very south of the world each year. Spot four.

Humpback whales sometimes leap right out of the water. Spot three.

Harp seal

Ringed seal

Ribbon seal

You can spot different seals by their markings. Find five of each of these.

Arctic skuas steal food from other birds. Spot two.

Puffins can use their wings like paddles to dive underwater for fish. Find three.

Killer whales catch seals by tipping up the ice so that they fall into the water. Spot three.

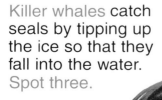

Little auks gather in groups called rafts, while they look for food. Find ten.

Blue whales are probably the largest creatures that ever lived. Spot one.

Dolphin handle

Find a gold cup with dolphin handles.

Hand blower

Divers use hand blowers to blow away sand and uncover treasure. Spot two.

Barrel

Jar

Food for the ship's crew was stored in jars and barrels like these. Spot six of each.

Sometimes a diver makes a sketch of the ship. Spot a diver sketching.

Pirate treasure

Pirates were looking for chests full of coins. Spot seven.

In the 16th century, Spanish ships called galleons sailed from the Americas to Spain laden with gold, silver and jewels. Many were attacked by pirates. These divers are exploring a ship that sank with all her treasure.

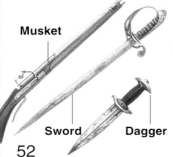

Musket

Sword **Dagger**

The ship's crew needed weapons to fight off the pirates. Find two of each of these.

Divers sometimes use metal detectors to help find buried treasure. Can you see one?

Find two gold plates.

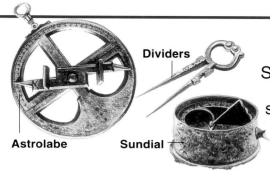

Astrolabe

Dividers

Sundial

Sailors navigated by the sun and stars. Find these measuring instruments.

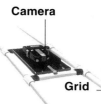

Camera

Grid

When divers find a wreck, they measure and photograph it. Can you see a camera?

Heavy things are attached to lifting bags which float to the surface. Find eight.

Silver ingot

Gold ingot

Gold and silver from South America were made into ingots in Mexico. Find seven silver and six gold ingots.

Small objects are brought to the surface in baskets. Can you spot six?

Find some divers measuring part of the wreck.

Cannon

Cannon-balls

The captain used this whistle to give orders to his crew. Can you find it?

Rich people sailed as passengers. Find these six jewels.

Gold locket

Rosary

Jewel encrusted buckle

Emerald ring

Emerald cross

Gold chain

Galleons built for battle had lots of cannons. Find 10 cannons and 20 cannonballs.

The big blue sea

Manta rays are huge but harmless. They feed on tiny animals called plankton. Spot six.

Spinner dolphins spin around in the air as they leap from the water. Spot ten.

Frigate birds steal food from other birds. Can you find two?

Divers study dangerous sharks from cages. Spot a diver in a cage.

Flying fish build up speed in the water and leap out to escape enemies. Spot seven.

A purse seine is a large circular net used to trap big shoals of fish. Can you see two?

Great white sharks, flying fish and many other huge, fast or dangerous creatures live right in the middle of the ocean. They swim close to the surface where there is more sunlight and plenty of food to eat.

Black and yellow sea snakes swim in groups. Spot 18 others.

Remoras hitch a lift on large fish and feed on their leftovers. Spot six.

Blue-striped marlins turn black or blue just before they eat. Find three.

Boobies fly across the water and dive down when they see a fish to eat. Spot six.

Great white sharks eat almost anything they find, even people. Spot three more.

Portuguese men-of-war have long trailing tentacles which are very poisonous. Spot five.

Sailfish are the fastest fish in the sea. Can you find one?

Yellow fin tuna often swim below dolphins. That's how fishermen sometimes find them. Spot six.

Dolphins can get caught in the nets by mistake. Spot five fishermen helping dolphins escape.

Leatherback turtles swim a long way to their breeding grounds. Spot four.

Whale sharks are the biggest sharks but they are not dangerous. Spot one.

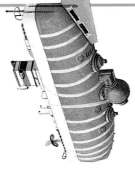

Nautile

Turtle

The abyss

The very deepest part of the ocean, called the abyss, is icy cold and dark. Explorers go down in small submarines, called submersibles. They have found volcanoes, hot springs, deep trenches, and some very strange creatures.

Sonar "fish" are towed by ships. They record what's on the ocean floor. Spot three.

Tripod fish walk along the sea floor on long fins like legs. Find one.

Bathyscaphes look like huge airships. They go into deep trenches. Can you see two?

Angler fish use a long fin with a light on the end to catch other fish. Can you see three?

Beardworms grow huge on food from the hot springs. Spot five groups.

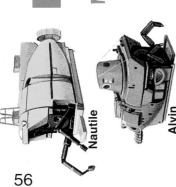

Submersibles need thick walls, to stop the water above from crushing them. Spot each of these.

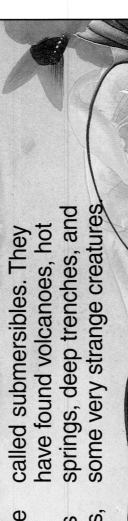
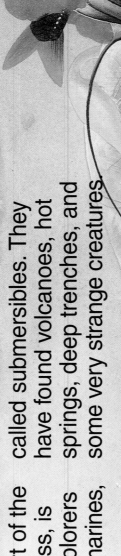

Deep sea spiders can be 50cm (20in) across. Can you see five?

Hatchet fish have two huge eyes on top of their heads. Spot 17.

Giant squid have huge eyes that are about 17 times the size of yours. Spot four.

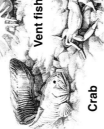

Anemone

Vent fish

Crab

These strange creatures live and feed around the smokers. Find 20 of each.

Deep Flight is a submersible for the future. It will fly to the bottom fast. Can you see it?

Viper fish unhinge their jaws to gulp down large fish whole. Spot two.

Lantern fish have lights all along their bodies. Find 22.

Submersibles and ROVs have manipulator arms for picking things up. Spot five more.

Tall chimneys called black smokers grow up around hot springs. Find 15.

Gulper eels swallow large fish with their wide mouths. Spot four.

Sperm whales dive deep for food, but they must swim to the surface to breathe. Can you find two?

ROVs are controlled by a cable from submersibles or ships. Can you see three?

Coral dives

Millions of people dive for fun, and Australia's Great Barrier Reef is one of the best places to explore. The reef is made from the skeletons of billions of tiny creatures called corals. Can you find 15 divers here?

Sea slugs are small but they have bright markings. Spot each of these.

Fins help divers swim smoothly. Spot three yellow pairs.

Giant clams grow very slowly and can live for a hundred years. Find two.

Flash light

Underwater cameras need strong flash lights. Can you see four?

Sea wasp

Cone shell

Olive sea snake

These creatures are so poisonous, they can kill a person. Find one of each.

Tank

Regulator

Divers breathe compressed air from tanks. Spot a diver with two tanks.

Can you find three blue snorkels?

Snorkel

Mask

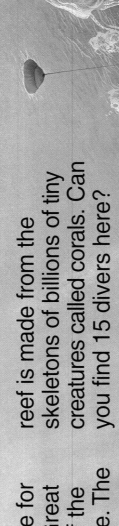

Can you find a leaking mask, half full of water?

"I'm OK"

"Let's go up"

Divers use hand signals to "talk" to each other. Spot two divers making each of these signals.

Sea fan

Staghorn coral

Brain coral

Corals are animals though some look more like rocks. Spot four clumps of each type.

Divers wear weights on their belts to help them descend. Find a diver with six weights.

Clown fish hide in poisonous anemones. Find nine others.

Barracudas are curious and sometimes follow a diver. Spot five.

Divers add air to jackets called BCs to go up, and let it out to go down. Spot a pink BC.

Hundreds of small fish live in the reef. Find three of each of these.

Surgeon fish

Clown Triggerfish

Moorish idol

Can you find four divers with knives?

Wetsuit

Knife

Can you see a diver in a short pink wetsuit like this one?

Air

Depth gauge

Consoles with dials show how much air is left and how deep it is. Find four.

Marker buoys on the surface show where the divers are. Can you see one?

59

Kelp forest

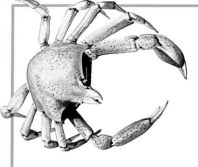

As kelp crabs get bigger, they shed their shell and grow a new one. Spot six.

Sea stars stand on tiptoe to shed their eggs. Can you find two?

Bat rays glide through the forest on wing-like fins. Can you see three?

Ocean goldfish guard their space in the kelp fiercely. Find 11.

Sea otters wrap up in kelp when they snooze on the surface. Find eight.

Giant kelp is the fastest growing plant in the world. It can grow 60cm (24in) in a day. Huge underwater kelp forests are home to thousands of creatures. People use the kelp too, to make things such as ice cream or paint.

Gray whales shelter in the kelp to keep their babies safe. Spot a mother and her baby.

Sea snails eat their way up kelp plants. Spot 17.

Californian sealions are speedy swimmers and like to play. Spot three.

60

Blacksmith

Halfmoon

Opaleye

These fish live in large groups. They feed on the kelp. Spot 15 of each.

Giant kelpfish look like pieces of kelp, so they are hard to see. Can you find six?

Giant octopuses grip their prey tightly with their strong tentacles. Find four.

Ships like this one harvest the kelp. Can you see the bottom of one?

Senoritas clean other fish and the kelp. Can you see five?

Abalones have beautiful shells. Spot one abalone and two empty shells.

Young

Female

Male

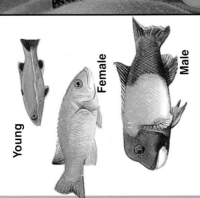

Male, female and young sheephead wrasses all look different. Spot three of each.

Hungry sea urchins destroy the kelp. Find six red and six purple ones.

Each kelp plant has a holdfast which clings to the rock. Can you see three others?

61

Oil rigs

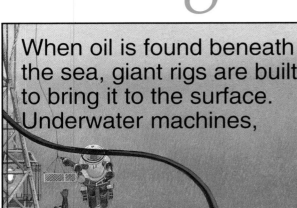

Helmets let divers see and breathe easily. Find one with a square face plate.

Face plate

Rigs are built on land and then towed out to sea. Can you find five of them?

Newtsuit

Hardsuits stop the water pushing in on the diver. The Newtsuit has legs with special joints. Find two.

Wasp

Wasp suits have propellers to help them move around in the water. Find five.

Conger eels have sharp teeth. They live in holes, so divers have to watch where they put their hands. Spot four.

When oil is found beneath the sea, giant rigs are built to bring it to the surface. Underwater machines, called ROVs, and deep sea divers check the rigs for damage and do repairs. It can be dangerous work.

Diving bells are used to lower divers into deep water. Can you find three?

Pipe-laying barge

Pipes are laid by these special barges. Find one pipe-laying barge.

Stinger

Pipe

Special rods are heated up to cut metal. Spot three divers cutting.

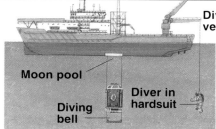

Some seals are fierce and try to chase divers away. Spot five.

Diving support vessel

Moon pool

Diving bell

Diver in hardsuit

Diving equipment is lowered into the water from a diving support vessel. Find one.

Airbags are used to support heavy things in the water. Spot ten.

Tools are lowered down from the surface in these baskets. Can you find five?

Work ROV

Different types of ROVs, (remotely operated vehicles) are used for each job. Work ROVs have mechanical arms. Spot three.

Eyeball ROV

Eyeball ROVs have cameras which video any damage and repairs. Spot six.

Gas

Hot water

Telephone line

Umbilicals join divers to a bell, bringing them gas and hot water. Spot six.

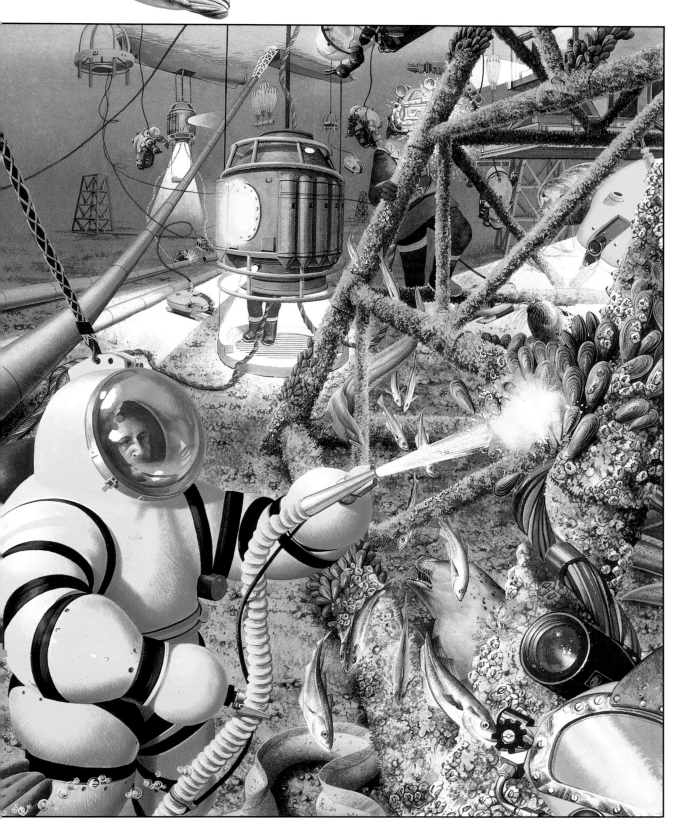

Mussels grow all over the rig and sometimes have to be cleaned off. Spot five groups.

Find 12 of each of these fish.

Pollack

Cod

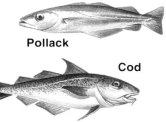

Water jet pumps are used for tasks such as cleaning. Can you see one?

Seaside jungle

Ospreys catch fish with their large feet and claws. Spot one.

The glossy ibis uses its long beak to catch shellfish, insects and even snakes. Spot four.

The tangled roots of mangrove trees make a perfect home for many creatures. These trees grow in hot parts of the world where a river meets the sea. Their long roots reach down into the water to help prop them up.

Otters paddle on the surface and dive down for food. Find three.

Soldier crabs can recognize each other by their bright blue shells. Spot 22.

Saltwater crocodiles are very dangerous and very large. Find three more.

Dog-headed sea snakes slither through the water hunting for fish and crabs. Spot seven.

Mudskippers can use their fins like arms to drag themselves along the mud. Spot 25.

The mangrove roots are a good place for shellfish to breed. Spot 21 of each of these.

Oyster

Chama

Young tripletail fish hide on their sides near the surface. They look like dead leaves. Spot 12.

Ocean creatures often visit the mangroves to feed on plants. Can you spot two turtles?

Crab-eating macaques use their strong teeth to open shellfish. Spot two more.

When kingfishers spot a fish, they plunge head first after it. Can you see five?

Proboscis monkeys enjoy a swim. They often dive into the water to cool off. Spot five.

Some mangrove seedlings float for a year before planting themselves in the mud. Find 14.

Unlike most frogs, crab-eating frogs are quite happy in salt water. Spot three.

Male fiddler crabs use their enormous claw to fight off rivals. Spot three.

Volcanic islands

Swallow-tailed gull. Spot four.

A few of these volcanic islands are still erupting. Can you find one?

Sealions surf in the waves for fun, but they must watch out for sharks. Find five.

Flightless cormorants hold their little wings out to dry after a dive. Spot one.

Common dolphin

Spotted dolphin

Dolphins come to the surface frequently for air. Find two of each of these types.

The Galápagos islands were formed by volcanoes erupting at the bottom of the sea. They are a very long way from any other land. Some of the creatures that live here are found nowhere else in the world.

Pelicans scoop up fish in the pouch under their beaks. Spot two.

Squid have two long arms and eight short ones. Find three.

A male frigate bird blows up his throat pouch to attract a mate. Spot two.

Pilot whales **nudge** their babies to the surface to breathe. Spot a mother and baby.

Albatrosses **live** mostly at sea. They only come to land to breed. Find one.

Fur seals **get too** hot in the midday sun, so they lie in the water to cool off. Spot two.

Red-footed booby

Blue-footed booby

Boobies **make** spectacular dives from 25m (82ft) high. Find four of each kind.

Sally lightfoot crabs **have red** shells and blue bellies. Can you see 25?

These penguins use their stubby wings to "fly" through the water. Spot eight.

Tiger sharks **hunt** alone. They swim all day, only stopping to eat. Can you find one?

Marine iguanas are lizards that can swim. They have to lie in the sun to warm up. Find 14 more.

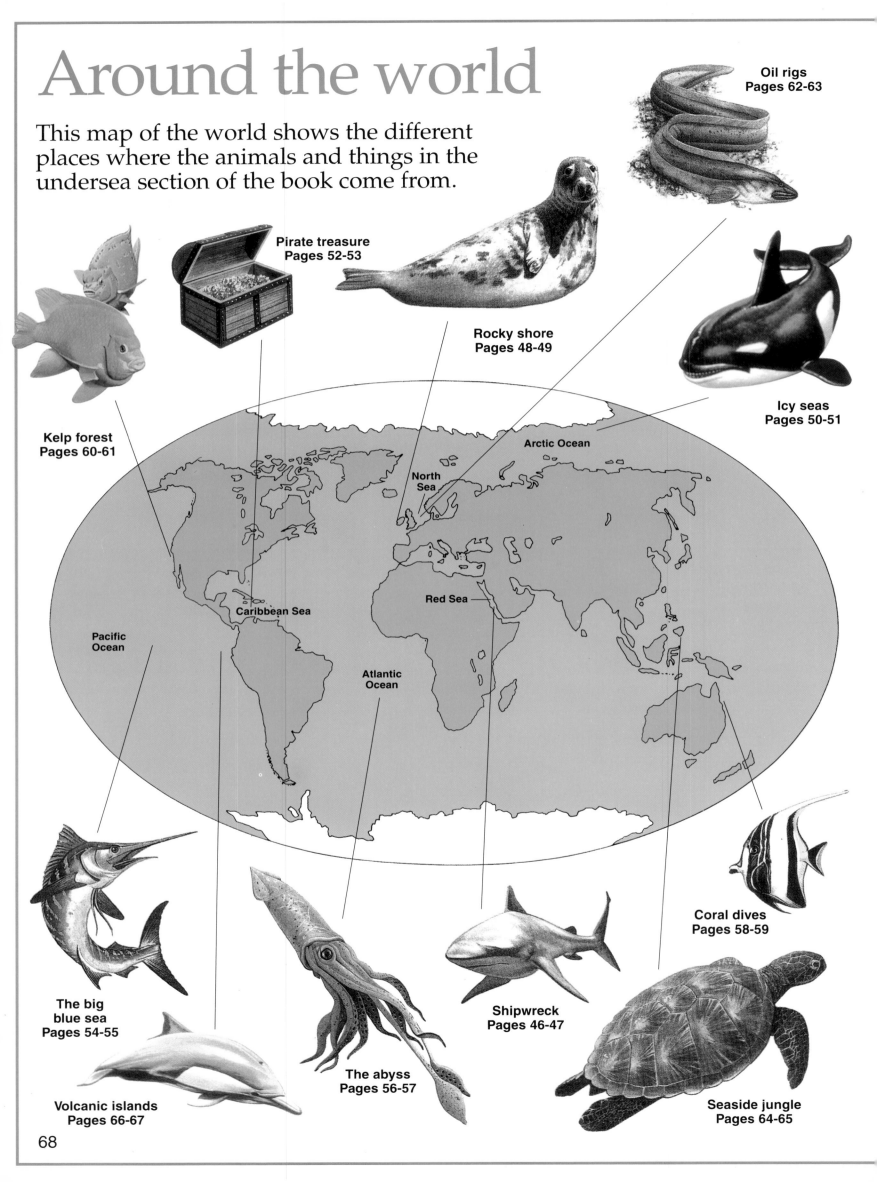

Around the world

This map of the world shows the different places where the animals and things in the undersea section of the book come from.

Oil rigs
Pages 62-63

Pirate treasure
Pages 52-53

Rocky shore
Pages 48-49

Icy seas
Pages 50-51

Kelp forest
Pages 60-61

Arctic Ocean

North
Sea

Caribbean Sea

Red Sea

Pacific
Ocean

Atlantic
Ocean

Coral dives
Pages 58-59

**The big
blue sea
Pages 54-55**

Shipwreck
Pages 46-47

Volcanic islands
Pages 66-67

The abyss
Pages 56-57

Seaside jungle
Pages 64-65

The Big Bug Search

The last part of this book looks at the wonderful world of bugs.
If you search hard on the next few pages, you'll find beautiful
beetles and butterflies, bird-eating spiders, slimy slugs and snails
and hundreds of other creepy-crawlies from all over the world.

Young bugs

Many of the bugs you'll see in this part of the book are adults, but some are young bugs, which look different from their parents. Young bugs are often called nymphs or larvae. They have to grow and change before they become adults. This is how a dragonfly grows up.

Nymph

Adult emerging

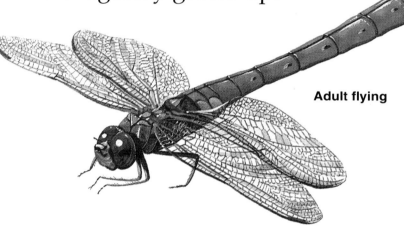

Adult flying

Dragonflies lay eggs in or near water. Each egg hatches into a dragonfly nymph.

As it grows, the nymph loses its skin. The last time it does this, it becomes an adult.

Extra hidden animals

As well as all the bugs, you'll find one of these animals hiding somewhere on each page in this part of the book. On pages which are split into two halves (pages 74-75, 86-87 and 90-91), there's one animal to find in each half.

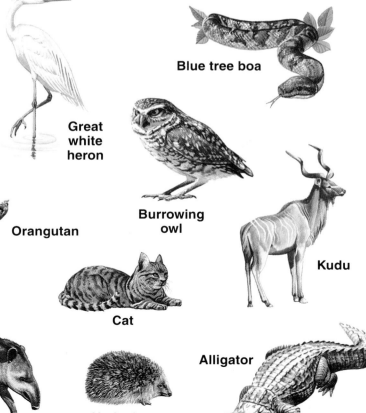

Great white heron

Blue tree boa

Burrowing owl

Orangutan

Kudu

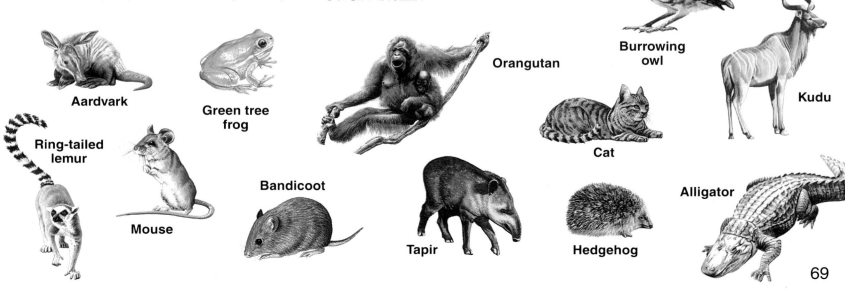

Aardvark

Green tree frog

Cat

Ring-tailed lemur

Mouse

Bandicoot

Tapir

Hedgehog

Alligator

Homes and gardens

Not all minibeasts live in wild places. Many live in gardens, parks, and even in and around houses. This is a picture of a house in Britain. Can you spot 158 creatures here?

Snails leave sticky trails which show where they have been. Can you track down ten?

Most fleas drink the blood of animals. Some drink human blood too. Spot ten.

Female garden spiders are bigger than males and often eat them after mating. Spot eight spiders.

Houseflies' mouths are like a mop, soaking up liquid food. Find ten houseflies.

Cinnabar moth

Caterpillar

Unlike most moths, cinnabar moths fly by day. Spot seven moths and six caterpillars.

Lacewings sleep somewhere warm all winter. They turn brown while they sleep. Find 14.

Cockroaches have flat bodies. They can squeeze under things to hide. Spot 11.

Only male common blue butterflies are really blue. Spot four of each sex.

Male

Female common blue butterfly

Honeybees carry yellow pollen from flowers in "baskets" on their back legs. Can you find ten?

Zebra spiders creep up behind their victims and pounce on them. Find five.

Their name means "100 feet" but no centipedes have that many. Can you spot six?

Wasps like anything sweet, including our food. They'll sting you if you annoy them. Spot 13.

Devil's coach-horses arch their bodies to scare off enemies. Spot six coach-horses.

Earwigs lift their fierce-looking tails if they are scared, but they can't hurt you. Spot nine.

Tail

Greenflies suck the juice out of plants for their food. Can you spot 17?

Spittle bugs blow air and spit out of their bottoms to make foam. Find eight bugs hidden in foam.

71

Cactus city

This dry desert in the north of Mexico doesn't look like a very comfortable home, but thousands of bugs live here. Many stay in cool underground burrows during the hot day.

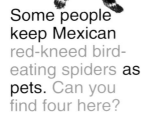

Some people keep Mexican red-kneed bird-eating spiders as pets. Can you find four here?

Painted grasshoppers are named after their bright-looking bodies. Can you spot ten?

Harvester ants collect seeds and store them deep underground. Find 15 busy ants.

Hercules beetles are some of the biggest insects in the world. Can you spot six?

Whip scorpions have a long, thin tail like a whip. It can't hurt you, though. Spot five.

Ant-lion larvae dig pits in the sand. When other bugs fall in, they eat them. Find three.

Find five lynx spiders.

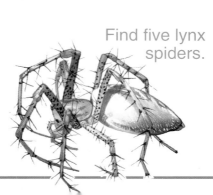

Tarantula hawk wasps lay their eggs on tarantula spiders' bodies. Can you find seven of them?

When insects pass a trapdoor spider's home, it flips up its "door" and grabs them. Spot four.

Scorpions lurk in cool burrows until the sun sets. Then they go hunting. Spot six.

Giant red velvet mites hatch out after rain and rush around looking for food. Spot ten.

Some honey ants hang upside down in the nest. Their tummies are full of honey. Spot 13.

Blister beetles sting your skin if you touch them. Find four blister beetles.

Yucca moths only lay their eggs in a yucca plant's flowers. Spot five yucca moths.

Tarantula. Find six.

A southern black widow spider will only bite you if you annoy it. Can you spot four?

73

Island paradise

The island of Madagascar is home to many bugs that aren't found anywhere else. The bugs on this page live in thick, dry woods. Those on the opposite page live in a rainforest.

Brilliant red dragonflies flit through the trees in the rainforest. Spot four.

Striped flatworms slither across the forest floor after it has rained. Can you find four?

Weevils often have long noses, but giraffe-necked weevils have long necks. Find four.

Huge emperor dragonflies catch insects flying past. Can you spot six of them?

Some stick insects grow fake 'moss' on their bodies as a disguise. Find three.

Thorn spiders look like prickly jewels in their huge webs. Find four.

Giant millipedes can be poisonous, so few animals eat them. Can you find five?

This praying mantis nymph is very well disguised. Can you spot four?

Green lynx spiders blend in with their leafy surroundings. Find four.

Pill millipedes can't run from enemies. They roll into a ball instead. Spot six.

Rosea bugs look a little like leaves. If a bird pecks one, the whole group flies off. Find 27.

Hairy weevils only live in Madagascar. Spot seven of each of these.

Longhorn beetles lay their eggs in dead wood. Later, their larvae eat it. Find seven.

Hissing cockroaches hiss by blowing air out of two holes in their tummies. Find five.

Can you find four shield bug adults and four nymphs?

Adult

Nymph

Spot six butterflies with their wings open and five with their wings shut.

Dazzling display

Some of the most beautiful insects in the world live in rainforests, but they are often hard to spot. Can you find 95 minibeasts in this rainforest in Peru, in South America?

Find nine leaf beetles.

A wandering spider's bite is so poisonous, it can kill a person. Can you find two?

Thornbugs look like thorns. Their disguise fools hungry birds. Spot ten.

When Hamadryas butterflies fly, their wings make clicking noises. Can you spot four?

Some assassin bugs have spiky bodies. Enemies find them hard to chew. Can you find seven?

Hawk moth caterpillars look pretty but taste nasty, so birds leave them alone. Spot five.

Many gorgeous grasshoppers live in these forests. Find three of each of these kinds.

Long-legged stilt bugs have long, skinny legs that look a little like stilts. Find five.

These bright bugs must taste good because local people eat them. Find six.

Male harlequin beetles guard females with their long front legs. Find seven harlequin beetles.

Female

Male

This grasshopper hides by staying still and hoping it looks like a stick. Spot three.

Bark bugs are hard to spot. They blend into the background. Find seven.

Morpho butterfly. Spot four.

Male Hercules beetles use their horns to push other males away. Spot four.

Leafcutter ants eat fungus. They help it grow by covering it with chewed leaves. Find 16.

Between the trees

All kinds of amazing bugs live in the thick eucalyptus forests of eastern Australia. Ants as big as your toes go marching past, and poisonous spiders lurk in dark corners.

Emperor gum moths only lay their eggs on eucalyptus trees. Find three.

Sawfly larvae wave their heads and spit bitter liquid at enemies. Find nine.

Female redback spiders are much more poisonous than males. Can you spot three?

Processionary moth caterpillars leave a long silk thread behind them. Find 11.

Fierce **Sydney funnel-web spiders** only live near the city of Sydney. Spot four.

Bulldog ants are the biggest, fiercest ants in the world. Can you spot 12 of them?

Giant **stick insects** unfold their wings to give enemies a shock. Can you find four?

Net throwing spiders throw a net of silk over their victims. Spot two more.

Some crickets flash their bright backs at enemies to scare them. Find five.

Bogong moths can eat whole fields of grain if they get together. Spot four.

Common grass yellow butterflies sip water from puddles in hot weather. Spot 23.

Emperor gum moth caterpillars have bright spikes to warn enemies off. Find four.

Gliding spiders can stretch out two flaps of skin and glide through the air. Find four.

Some people dig moth caterpillars called "witchetty grubs" out of tree trunks and eat them. Find six.

There are over 450 different types of shield bugs in Australia. Spot nine of this kind.

Monarch butterflies can fly up to 130km (80 miles) in one day. Find five.

Water world

Ponds are perfect homes for many small creatures. They are often nurseries for young insects too. Can you spot 121 minibeasts in this North American pond?

Fisher spiders crawl down plants, catch fish, then haul them up to eat. Spot eight.

Tube

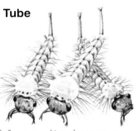

Mosquito larvae dangle under the surface of the pond. They breathe through a tube. Spot seven.

Backswimmers swim upside down, using their back legs as oars. Find six.

Stoneflies can't fly well, so they sit beside the water most of the time. Spot nine.

Damselflies can't walk well. They use their legs to grab hold of plants. Spot seven.

Water striders skim lightly across the surface of the pond. Spot eight water striders.

Fishermen put fake caddisflies on their hooks to attract fish. Spot six real caddisflies.

Pond snails do a very useful job. They eat plants and make the water much clearer. Find 11.

Great diving beetle larvae bite their victims and then suck out their insides. Find five.

Water scorpions lurk just below the surface, grabbing passing insects. Spot six.

Dragonfly nymphs have jaws that shoot out to crunch up food. Can you spot five?

Caddisfly larvae are safe inside a case covered with pebbles and shells. Find five.

Whirligig beetles can look into the air and under the water at the same time. Find 15.

Great diving beetles have strong back legs to help them swim and dive. Spot ten.

Water stick insects breathe air through a narrow breathing tube. Find five stick insects.

Adult mayflies never eat. They just mate, lay eggs and die. Find nine.

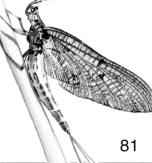

81

In the woods

If you walked through this wood in northern France, thousands of eyes might be watching you. Tiny creatures make their homes up in the trees, or down on the ground.

Male stag beetles fight with their sharp antlers, but rarely hurt each other. Find six.

Wood ants squirt acid out of their bottoms to attack enemies. Can you spot 20?

Crane flies have six legs. They can survive losing one or two of them. Find eight.

Hedge snails are easy for birds to spot, so they try to stay hidden. Find six snails.

Darter dragonflies flit through the trees in woodland clearings. Can you spot three?

Male empid flies give females a bug wrapped in silk while they mate. Find 12.

Bumblebees fly from flower to flower, collecting pollen. Spot four bumblebees.

Longhorn beetles don't have horns, just long antennae that look like them. Can you spot seven?

Antennae

Burying beetles lay their eggs next to a dead animal. When the eggs hatch into larvae, they eat it. Spot ten.

Hornets chew bark to make a soggy mixture. They use it to build nests. Find four.

The amount of purple you can see on a purple emperor butterfly's wings depends on the light. Spot six.

Bark beetles lay their eggs in tree bark. When the eggs hatch, the larvae eat the bark. Find 11.

Large black slugs slither along the woodland floor, leaving a slimy trail. Spot seven.

Poplar hawk moths can see in the dark, so they fly at night. Find five.

Male horseflies drink plant juices, but females need to drink animals' blood. Spot four.

Crab spiders lie in wait for insects in flowers. Then they attack and kill them. Spot three.

Swamp life

Lots of bugs live together in the dark, murky water of the Everglades swamp in Florida.

There are pools of fresh water and patches of salt water, with different bugs in each.

Golden orb weaver spiders spin huge webs above the water. Spot three.

Eggs

Apple snails climb out of the water to lay eggs. Find six snails and three clumps of eggs.

Io moths have markings like eyes on their wings. They flash them at enemies. Spot five.

Male fiddler crabs wave their big front claw to look fierce. Find five more.

Huge swarms of mosquitoes live here. They can give people painful bites. Spot 14.

Jumping spider. Spot three.

Tree snails' shells can have over 40 patterns. Can you spot two of each of these?

Viceroy butterflies drink sweet liquid called nectar from plants. Can you see five?

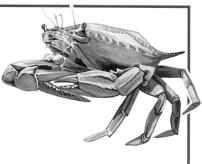

Blue land crabs scuttle along the mangrove tree roots. Can you find 14?

Green darner dragonflies swoop over the water, looking for insects to eat. Find five.

A lubber grasshopper's thick skin protects it from enemies' teeth. Find four.

Fisher spiders always find plenty to eat in the Everglades. Can you find three?

Female giant water bugs stick eggs onto males' backs. Spot three males and a female.

Midge larvae float in the water, eating tiny bugs. Spot seven midge larvae.

Zebra butterflies lay their eggs on passionflower leaves. Can you see four?

85

Deep in the jungle

The jungles of southeast Asia are as busy by night as they are by day. The left-hand page shows who comes out in the daytime and the right-hand page shows the night.

Hairy bird-eating spiders really do eat birds. They can climb trees too. Find four.

Fireflies' tummies light up, then flash on and off. Find 11.

Cockchafer beetle. Find seven.

Stay away from red centipedes. Their bites are very painful. Can you spot five?

Atlas moths are the largest moths in the world. Look hard and try to find three.

Snails slither around the jungle. Find three of each of these two kinds of snails.

Longicorn beetles use their long feelers to explore the jungle. Can you see five?

Loepa moths have no tongues. They don't live long enough to need food. Find four.

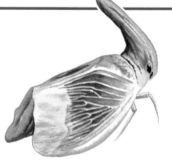

Lantern bugs got their name because they often flutter around people's lanterns. Spot ten.

Flat-backed millipedes eat fungi that grows on trees. Can you find five of them?

These shield bugs taste horrible, so other animals don't eat them. Find seven.

Brilliant jewel beetles like lying on leaves in the warm sunshine. Find eight.

Termites march to and fro on the jungle floor. Can you spot 16 termites here?

Male cicadas make a chirping sound with a part of their tummies. Find five.

Birdwing butterflies are as big as a hand when their wings are open. Spot four.

Weaver ants make nests by sticking leaves together with spit. Spot 12.

Nephila spiders spin webs out of pale yellow silk. Can you spot four of them?

Minibeast safari

People go on expeditions, or safaris, to see the wildlife of Africa. They may not see the thousands of bugs that live there too. Spot 118 in this picture of part of South Africa.

Male rhinoceros beetles have a horn like a rhinoceros. Can you see five?

Tsetse flies drink other creatures' blood through a tube-shaped mouth. Find ten.

Swallowtail butterfly

Caterpillar

Swallowtail butterfly caterpillars wave smelly horns at enemies. Spot five caterpillars and three butterflies.

Potter wasps put caterpillars in their nests as food for their larvae. Find five potter wasps.

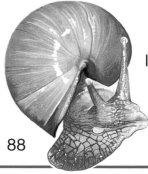

African land snails are the largest snails in the world. Can you spot four?

African assassin bugs work as a team, killing other insects. Find five.

Longhorn beetles chew their way into tree trunks. Find seven longhorn beetles.

African moon moths flash the eye-like markings on their wings at enemies. Spot three.

Hanging flies hang upside down from twigs with their long, skinny legs. Find eight.

Monarch butterflies eat plants that make their flesh taste horrible. Find four.

Histerid beetles like eating dung, or the bodies of dead animals. Find 21.

Ground beetles can squirt burning acid out of their bottoms. Can you spot four?

Processionary moth. Find three.

Processionary moth caterpillars wriggle along the ground in a long line. Spot ten.

Stalk-eyed flies got their name from their eyes. It's easy to see why. Find four.

A swarm of hungry locusts can eat a whole crop in hours. Spot 11 locusts.

If you disturb a praying mantis, it might wave its back wings at you. Spot six.

Insect city

Termites live in huge family groups. They build a mound of mud, spit and dung, and make a nest inside. This is what the nest looks like.

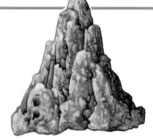

Termite mound

Only the queen termite lays eggs. She can lay over 30,000 a day. Can you find her?

All the king termite does is mate with the queen. Can you spot him?

Worker

Eggs

Worker termites take eggs to parts of the nest called nurseries. Find four nurseries.

Worker

Larvae

The eggs hatch into pale larvae. Worker termites care for them. Find 23 larvae.

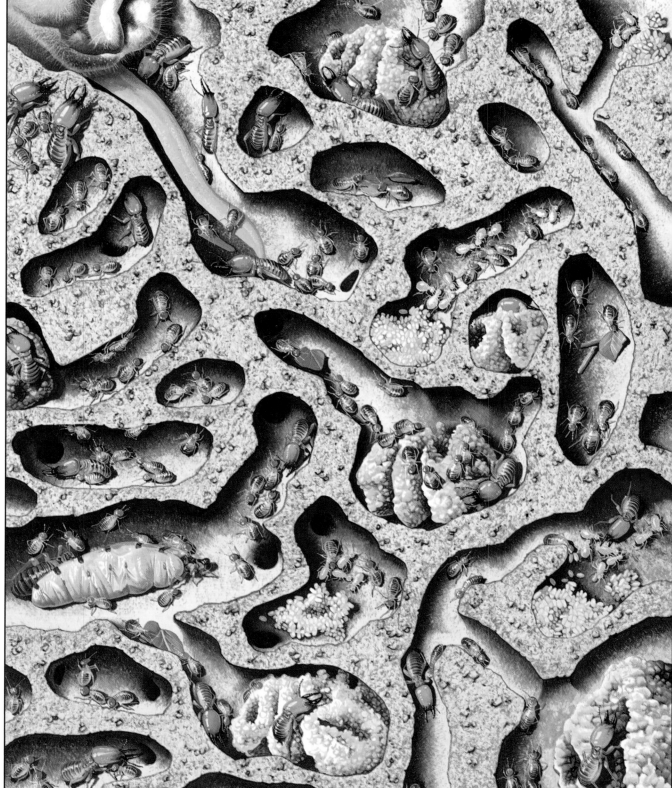

Soldier termites keep guard. They bite enemies, or squirt liquid at them. Spot 20.

Workers carry leaves into the nest in their mouths. Spot seven doing this job.

Fungus grows in "fungus gardens" in the nest. The termites eat it. Find six gardens.

Busy beehive

People keep honeybees in hives. The bees collect nectar and pollen from flowers. They eat the pollen and make the nectar into honey.

Beehive

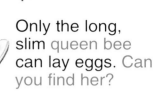

Only the long, slim queen bee can lay eggs. Can you find her?

Drones are big male bees. They mate with the queen, then get pushed out of the hive. Find seven.

Huddling around the queen to keep her safe.

Carrying balls of pollen on their back legs.

Feeding larvae that are growing in the hive.

Worker bees do several jobs. Find three workers doing each of these things.

Bees build little wax boxes called cells in the hive. Spot the cells being used for these things.

Find 17 cells with larvae in them.

Find ten cells full of pollen.

Find 14 cells full of honey.

Find 12 cells with bee eggs in them.

Worker bees sometimes spit food into another bee's mouth. Find one doing this.

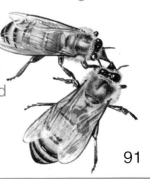

Around the world

This map of the world shows the places where all the bugs in this part of the book live.

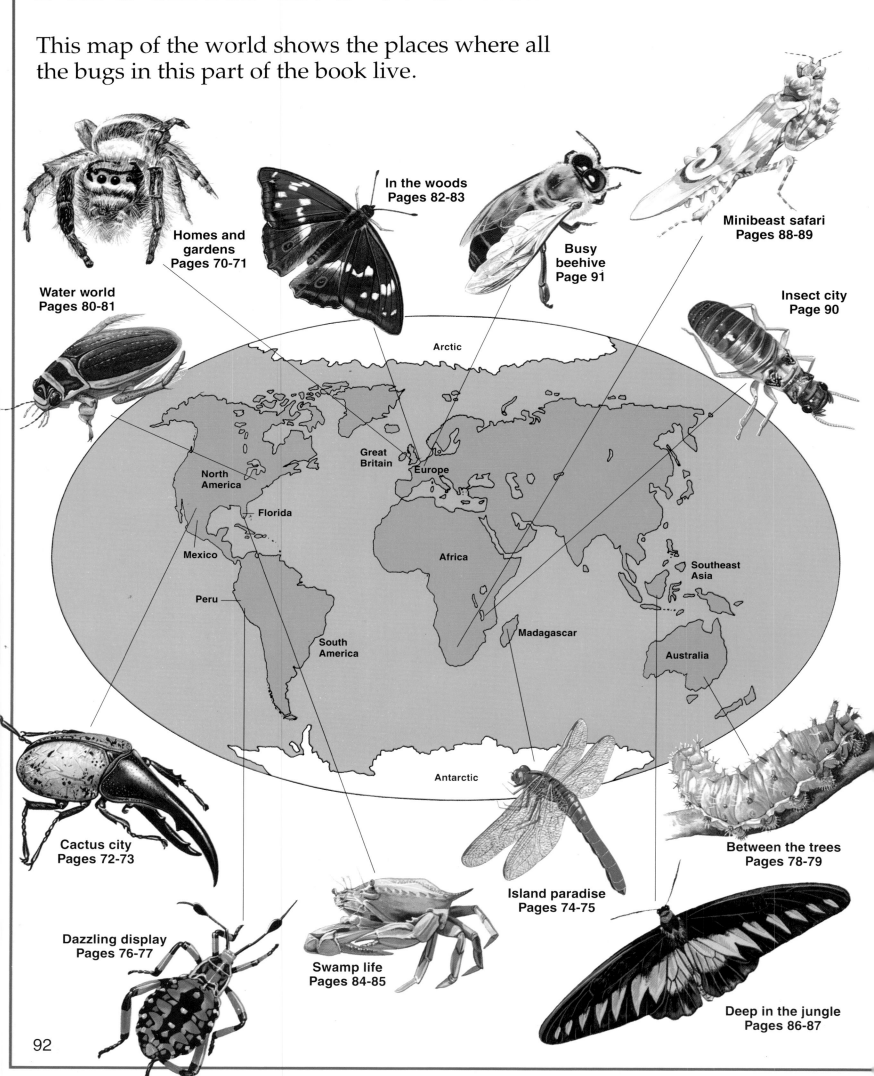

In the woods
Pages 82-83

Homes and gardens
Pages 70-71

Busy beehive
Page 91

Minibeast safari
Pages 88-89

Water world
Pages 80-81

Insect city
Page 90

Arctic

Great
Britain

Europe

North
America

Florida

Mexico

Africa

Peru

Southeast
Asia

South
America

Madagascar

Australia

Antarctic

Cactus city
Pages 72-73

Between the trees
Pages 78-79

Dazzling display
Pages 76-77

Island paradise
Pages 74-75

Swamp life
Pages 84-85

Deep in the jungle
Pages 86-87

Answers

The following pages show the answers to the puzzles. If you get stuck and want to find out where something is, look through them and find the name and the page numbers of the puzzle you are doing.

For example, if you wanted to find out where the Styracosaurus was on the "Back in time" puzzle, first you'd look for the "Back in time" answers (which are on page 94). What you'd see is a key like the one below.

Each key shows the outlines of the animals. Each outline has a number. The numbers are also shown after the animals' names in a list next to the key. Look for "Styracosaurus" in the list and find its number.

Name of puzzle   Page numbers

This key shows the answers to the puzzle on pages 6-7.

List of animals and their numbers. The Styracosaurus is number 5.

Back in time 6-7

Alamosaurus 1 2
Deinosuchus 3 4
Styracosaurus 5
Ankylosaurus 6 7
Quetzalcoatlus 8 9
Stegosaurus 10 11
Panoplosaurus
12 13 14 15 16
Anatosaurus
17 18 19
Dromaeosaurus
20 21 22 23 24 25
Triceratops 26 27
Corythosaurus
28 29 30 31
Maiasaura 32
Pachycephalosaurus
33 34 35
Struthiomimus
36 37 38 39 40
41 42
Parasaurolophus
43 44 45
Pteranodon
46 47 48
Tyrannosaurus
49 50 51

The Styracosaurus is here (number 5).

There are 3 Pteranodons to find. Their numbers are 46, 47 and 48. Can you find them on this key?

To find out where the Styracosaurus is, look for 5 on the key. It is on the outline of the Styracosaurus and shows its position in the big picture.

Now you can look back to page 7 to see where the Styracosaurus is in the big picture. It is just to the left of the big Tyrannosaurus 51 and below Quetzalcoatlus 8.

When there are several animals of one kind to find, each of them has a number.

Back in time 6-7

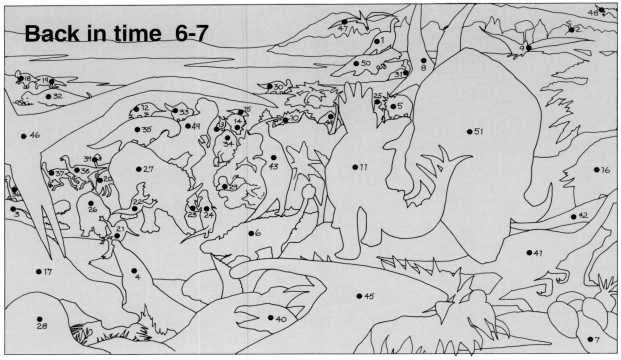

Alamosaurus 1 2
Deinosuchus 3 4
Styracosaurus 5
Ankylosaurus 6 7
Quetzalcoatlus 8 9
Stegosaurus 10 11
Panoplosaurus
12 13 14 15 16
Anatosaurus
17 18 19
Dromaeosaurus
20 21 22 23 24 25
Triceratops 26 27
Corythosaurus
28 29 30 31
Maiasaura 32
Pachycephalosaurus
33 34 35
Struthiomimus
36 37 38 39 40
41 42
Parasaurolophus
43 44 45
Pteranodon
46 47 48
Tyrannosaurus
49 50 51

Conifer forests 8-9

Skunks 1 2 3
Long-eared owls
4 5 6 7
Beavers 8 9 10
11 12 13 14 15
Crossbills 16 17
Moose
18 19 20 21 22 23
Fishers
24 25 26 27
Brown bears
28 29 30
Flying squirrels
31 32 33 34 35
Mink 36 37 38
Porcupines
39 40 41
Ospreys 42 43 44
Pumas 45 46 47
Northern shrikes
48 49
Chipmunks 50 51
52 53 54 55 56 57
Martens 58 59 60
Wolverines
61 62 63
Spruce grouse
64 65 66 67
Lynxes 68 69 70
Snowshoe hares
71 72 73 74 75 76
Black bears
77 78 79 80

Steamy swamps 10-11

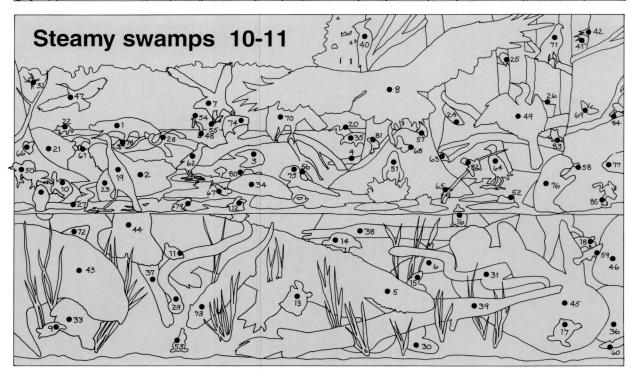

Alligators
1 2 3 4 5 6
Bald eagles 7 8
Terrapins
9 10 11 12 13
14 15 16 17 18
Little blue herons
19 20
Raccoons
21 22 23 24 25 26
Cottonmouth
snakes
27 28 29 30 31
Orb web spider 32
Snapping turtles
33 34 35 36
Garpikes 37 38 39
Pileated
woodpeckers
40 41 42
Manatees
43 44 45 46
Anhingas
47 48 49
Bullfrogs 50 51 52
Gambusia fish
53 54 55 56 57
58 59 60
Gallinules
61 62 63 64
Fisher spider 65
Zebra butterfly
66 67 68 69
Snail kites 70 71

Otters 72 73 74
75 76 77
Green tree frogs
78 79 80 81 82
83 84 85

Dusty deserts 12-13

The Arctic 14-15

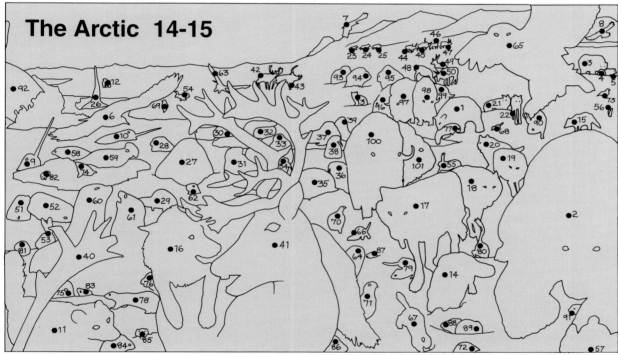

Under the sea 16-17

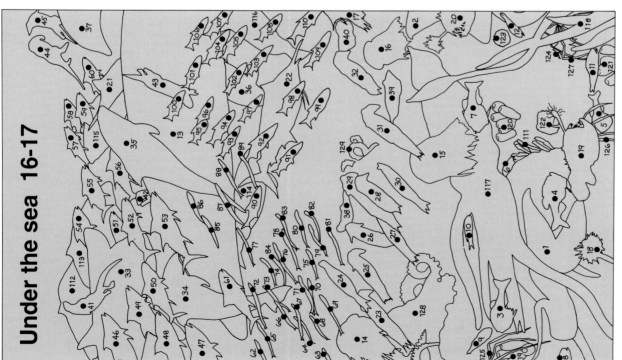

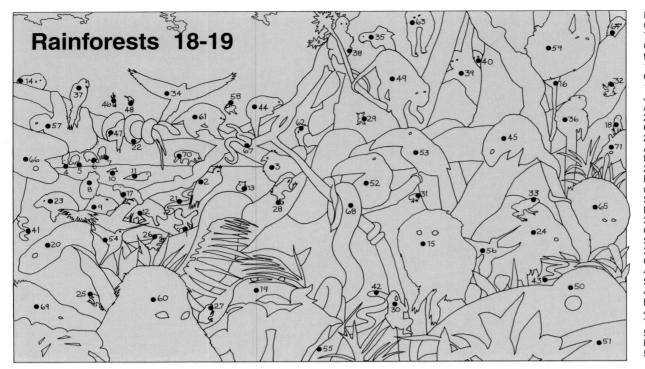

Rainforests 18-19

Hoatzins 1 2 3
Capybaras 4 5 6
7 8 9 10 11 12 13
Golden lion
tamarins
14 15 16
Cocks-of-the-rock
17 18
Jaguar 19
Anacondas
20 21 22
Giant armadillos
23 24
Arrow-poison
frogs 25 26 27 28
29 30 31 32 33
Blue and yellow
macaw 34
Scarlet macaw 35
Hyacinth macaw
36
Golden conure 37
Spider monkeys
38 39 40
Coral snakes
41 42 43
Silky anteaters
44 45
Howler monkeys
46 47 48 49
Toucans
50 51 52 53
Hummingbirds
54 55 56

Sloths 57 58 59
Uakari monkeys
60 61 62
63 64 65
Emerald tree
boas 66 67 68
Tapirs 69 70 71

Hot and dry 20-21

Camels
1 2 3 4 5 6 7 8 9
Desert
centipedes
10 11 12
Sandgrouse
13 14 15 16
Darkling beetles
17 18 19
Skinks
20 21 22 23
Tiger beetles
24 25 26
Toad-headed
lizards
27 28 29 30
Sand cats
31 32 33 34
Desert locusts
35 36 37 38
Sidewinders
39 40 41 42
Scorpions
43 44 45
Sand rats
46 47 48
Lanner falcons
49 50
Oryxes
51 52 53 54 55
56 57 58 59 60
Addaxes
61 62 63 64 65

Barbary sheep
66 67 68 69 70
71 72 73 74 75
76 77 78 79 80
81 82 83 84 85
Dorcas gazelles
86 87 88 89 90
91 92 93
Sand vipers
94 95 96 97
Jerboas 98 99
100 101 102
Sahara gecko
103
Coursers
104 105 106 107
Desert hares
108 109 110 111
Mauritanian toad
112
Desert
hedgehogs
113 114 115 116
Little owls
117 118 119 120
Fennec foxes
121 122 123 124

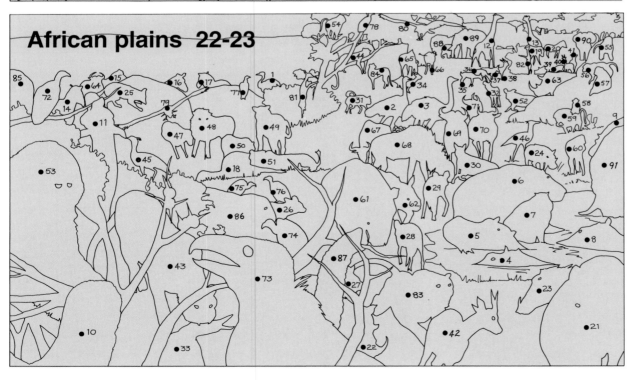

African plains 22-23

Ostriches 1 2 3
Hippos
4 5 6 7 8 9
Giraffes
10 11 12 13
Zebras 14 15 16
17 18 19 20 21
Warthogs
22 23 24
Wild dogs 25 26
27 28 29 30 31 32
Thomson's
gazelles
33 34 35 36 37
38 39 40 41 42
Leopards 43 44
Kori bustards
45 46
Lions
47 48 49 50 51 52
Baboons 53 54
55 56 57 58 59 60
Rhinos 61 62 63
Wildebeest 64 65
66 67 68 69 70 71
Vultures 72 73 74
75 76 77 78 79 80
Gerenuks 81 82
Cheetahs 83 84
Elephants 85 86
87 88 89 90 91

Hidden homes 24-25

Mole 1
Woodpeckers 2 3 4 5
Rabbits 6 7 8 9 10 11 12 13 14
Badgers 15 16 17 18
Nightjars 19 20
Squirrels 21 22 23 24
Tawny owls 25 26 27
Hedgehogs 28 29 30 31
Stag beetles 32 33
Horseshoe bats 34 35 36 37 38 39 40 41 42 43
Foxes 44 45 46 47 48
Jays 49 50 51 52
Shrews 53 54 55 56 57 58 59 60 61 62
Wild boars 63 64 65 66 67 68 69 70
Dormice 71 72 73 74 75
Magpies 76 77
Weasels 78 79 80 81
Fallow deer 82 83 84 85 86 87

By the sea 26-27

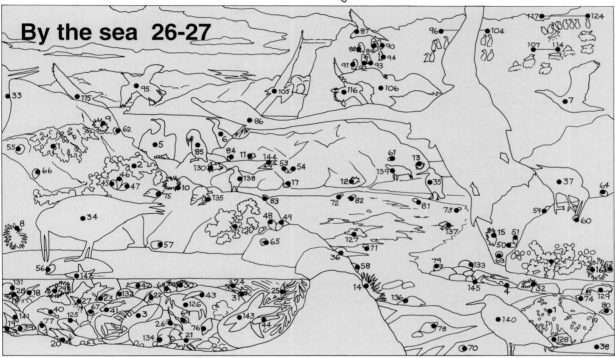

Sandhoppers 1
Barnacles 2
Lobsters 3 4
Cormorants 5 6 7
Snakelocks anemones 8 9 10 11 12 13 14 15 16 17
Prawns 18 19 20 21 22 23 24 25 26 27
Beadlet anemones 28 29 30 31 32
Oystercatchers 33 34 35 36 37 38
Blennies 39 40 41 42 43 44
Mussels 45 46 47 48 49 50 51 52 53 54
Limpets 55 56 57 58 59 60 61 62 63 64
Periwinkles 65 66 67 68 69 70 71 72 73 74
Dog whelks 75 76 77 78 79 80 81 82 83 84
Puffins 85 86 87 88 89 90 91 92 93 94

Guillemots 95 96 97 98 99 100 101 102 103 104
Kittiwakes 105 106 107 108 109 110 111 112 113 114
Razorbills 115 116 117 118 119 120 121 122 123 124
Crabs 125 126 127 128 129 130
Sea urchins 131 132 133
Hermit crabs 134 135 136 137
Redshanks 138 139 140
Starfish 141 142 143 144 145

Mountains 28-29

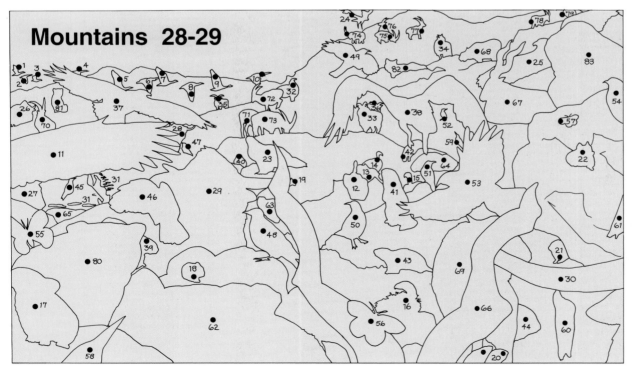

Bar-headed geese 1 2 3 4 5 6 7 8 9 10
Griffon vultures 11 12 13 14 15 16
Pikas 17 18 19 20 21 22
Lammergeiers 23 24 25
Yaks 26 27 28 29 30
Yeti/abominable snowman footprints 31
Tahrs 32 33 34
Bharals 35 36
Golden eagles 37 38
Marmots 39 40 41 42 43 44
Alpine choughs 45 46 47 48 49 50 51 52 53 54
Apollo butterflies 55 56 57
Wallcreepers 58 59 60 61
Black bears 62 63 64
Markhors 65 66 67
Takins 68 69
Ibexes 70 71 72

73 74 75 76 77 78 79
Snow leopards 80 81 82 83

Light and dark 30-31

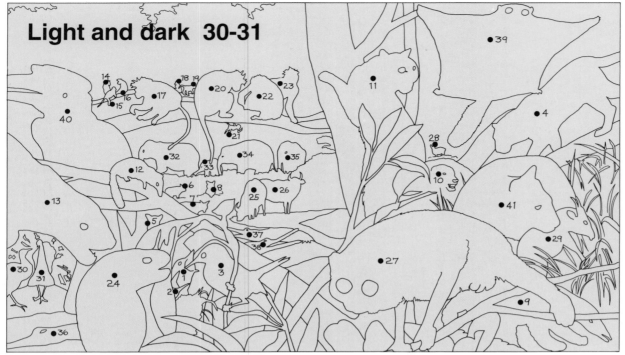

Tailor-birds
1 2 3
Leopard 4
Dholes 5 6 7 8
Pangolin 9
Sloth bear 10
Leopard cat 11
Madras tree shrew
12
Mongoose 13
Macaques
14 15 16 17 18 19
20 21 22 23
King cobra 24
Gaurs 25 26
Slender loris 27
Muntjac deer
28 29
Peacock/peahen
30 31
Elephants
32 33 34 35
Gavials
36 37 38
Giant flying
squirrel 39
Hornbill 40
Tiger 41

Magical world 32-33

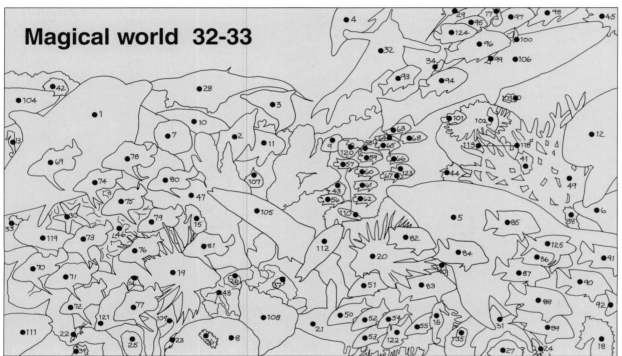

Bottlenose
dolphins
1 2 3 4 5 6
Sea sponges
7 8 9
Dugongs
10 11 12
Sea horses 13
14 15 16 17 18
Lion fish 19 20
Wobbegong 21
Flame shrimps
22 23 24
Tiger cowries
25 26 27
Manta rays
28 29
Blue sea stars
30 31
Hammerhead
shark 32
Naked sea slugs
33 34 35
Sacoglossan
sea slugs
36 37 38
Spanish dancers
39 40 41
Crown of thorns
42 43 44 45
Brain coral 46
Sea fan 47
Plate coral 48
Staghorn coral 49

Snappers 50 51
52 53 54 55
Angelfish
56 57 58 59 60
61 62 63 64 65
66 67 68
Damselfish
69 70 71 72 73
74 75 76 77 78
79 80 81
Red emperors
82 83 84 85 86
87 88 89 90 91
92
Sweetlips 93 94
95 96 97 98
Wrasses 99 100
Clown fish
101 102 103
Barracudas
104 105 106
Stone fish
107 108
Sea cucumber
109 110
Parrot fish
111 112
Sea squirts
113 114 115 116
117 118
Giant clams
119 120
'Odd' fish 121
122 123 124 125

Out and about 34-35

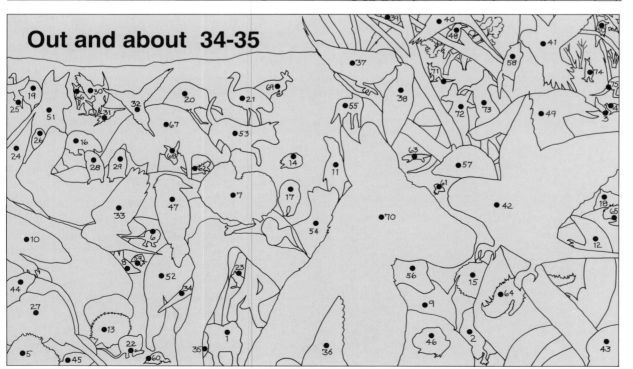

Shingle-backed
skinks 1 2
Mallee fowl 3 4
Frilled lizards
5 6 7
Bandicoots 8 9
Goannas 10 11 12
Echidnas 13 14 15
Wombats 16 17 18
Emus 19 20 21
Hopping mice
22 23
Budgerigars/
parakeets 24 25
26 27 28 29 30 31
32 33 34 35 36 37
38 39 40 41 42 43
Water-holding
frogs 44 45 46
Kookaburras
47 48 49 50
Dingos
51 52 53 54 55 56
Quolls 57 58
Marsupial moles
59 60 61
Thorny devils
62 63 64 65
Kangaroos
66 67 68 69 70
71 72 73 74 75

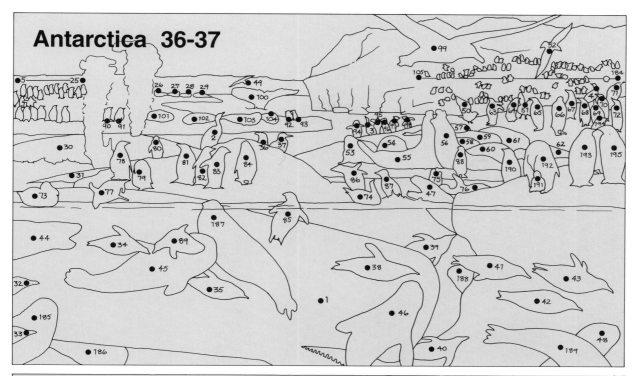

Antarctica 36-37

A closer look 38-39

On the farm 40-41

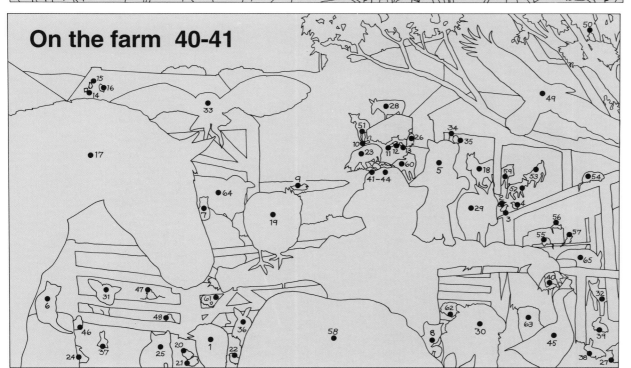

Prehistoric seas 44-45

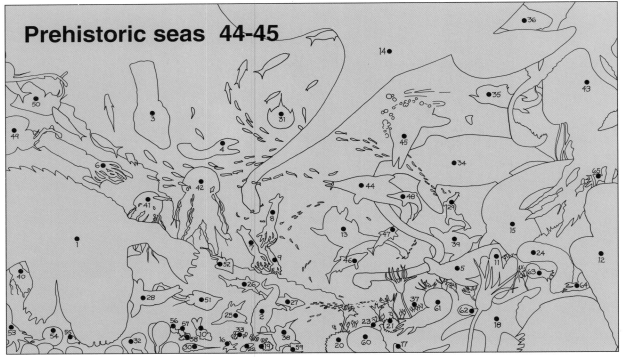

Placodus 1 2
Tanystropheus 3 4
Pliosaurus 5
Belemnites 6 7 8 9
Sponges 10 11 12
Plesiosaurus 13 14 15
Starfish 16 17 18
Sea urchins 19 20 21
Sea cucumbers 22 23 24
Sharks 25 26 27
Geosaurus 28 29
King crabs 30 31
Lampshells 32 33
Elasmosaurus 34
Rabbit fish 35 36
Sea lilies 37
Archelon 38 39
Jellyfish 40 41 42 43
Ichthyosaurus:
  adults 44 45
  babies 46 47 48
Banjo fish 49 50 51 52
Ammonites 53 54 55 56 57 58 59 60 61 62 63 64 65

Shipwreck 46-47

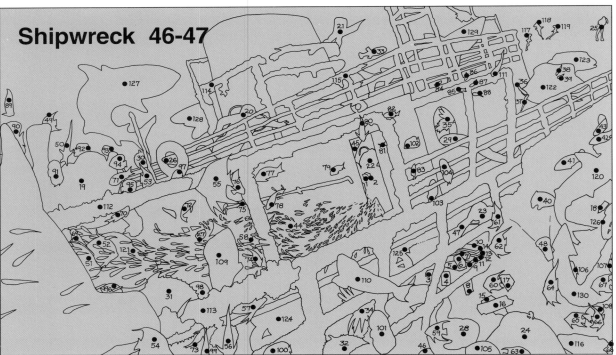

Gold bars 1 2 3 4 5 6 7 8 9 10 11 12 13 14 15 16 17 18
Divers 19 20 21 22 23 24 25
Moray eels 26 27 28 29
Puffer fish 30 31 32 33
Lion fish 34 35
Cleaner fish 36 37 38 39
Blue spotted groupers 40 41 42 43
Glass fish 44
Flashlights 45 46 47 48
Angel fish 49 50 51 52 53 54 55 56 57 58 59 60 61 62 63 64 65 66 67 68
Anthias 69 70 71 72 73 74 75 76 77 78 79 80 81 82 83 84 85 86 87 88
Butterfly fish 89 90 91 92 93 94 95 96 97 98 99 100 101 102 103 104 105 106 107 108

Parrot fish 109 110 111
Pink corals 112 113 114 115
Crocodile fish 116
Hammerhead sharks 117 118 119 120
Napoleon wrasses 121 122 123
Bikes 124 125 126
Reef sharks 127 128 129
Anchor 130

Rocky shore 48-49

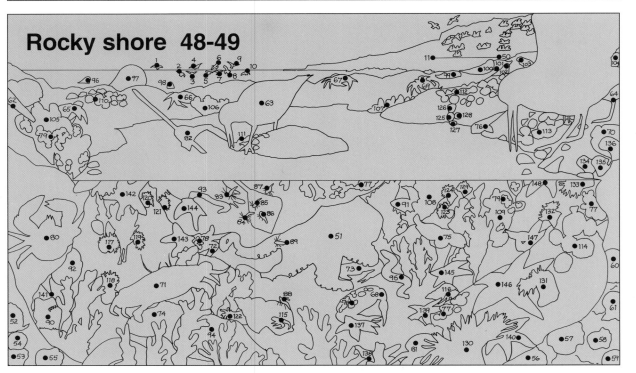

Kittiwakes 1 2 3 4 5 6 7 8 9 10 11 12 13 14 15 16 17 18 19 20 21 22 23 24 25 26 27 28 29 30 31 32 33 34 35 36 37 38 39 40 41 42 43 44 45 46 47 48 49 50
Octopus 51
Ammonites 52 53 54 55 56 57 58 59 60 61
Oystercatchers 62 63 64
Shore crabs 65 66 67
Edible crabs 68 69 70
Velvet swimming crabs 71 72 73
Blennies 74 75 76
Barnacles on rocks 77
Barnacles on crabs 78
Barnacles on mussels 79
Squat lobsters 80 81
Net and bucket 82

Prawns 83 84 85 86 87 88 89
Rock gobies 90 91
Butterfish 92 93 94 95
Grey seals 96 97 98 99 100 101 102 103 104
Mussels 105 106 107 108 109
Limpets 110 111 112 113 114
Hermit crabs 115 116
Beadlet anemones 117 118 119 120 121 122 123 124 125 126 127 128 129 130 131 132 133 134 135 136
"Bloody Henry" starfish 137 138 139 140
Cushion star 141 142 143 144
Common starfish 145 146 147 148

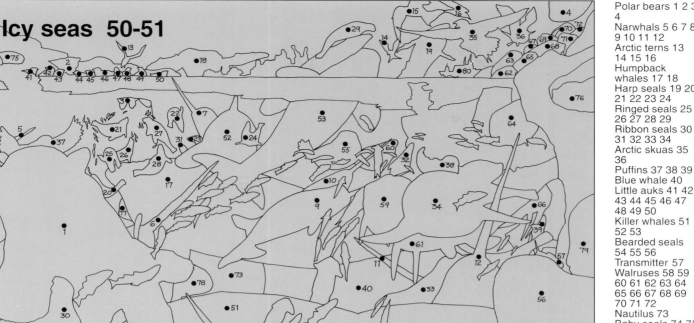

Icy seas 50-51

Polar bears 1 2 3 4
Narwhals 5 6 7 8 9 10 11 12
Arctic terns 13 14 15 16
Humpback whales 17 18
Harp seals 19 20 21 22 23 24
Ringed seals 25 26 27 28 29
Ribbon seals 30 31 32 33 34
Arctic skuas 35 36
Puffins 37 38 39
Blue whale 40
Little auks 41 42 43 44 45 46 47 48 49 50
Killer whales 51 52 53
Bearded seals 54 55 56
Transmitter 57
Walruses 58 59 60 61 62 63 64 65 66 67 68 69 70 71 72
Nautilus 73
Baby seals 74 75 76

Beluga whales 77 78 79
Research ship 80

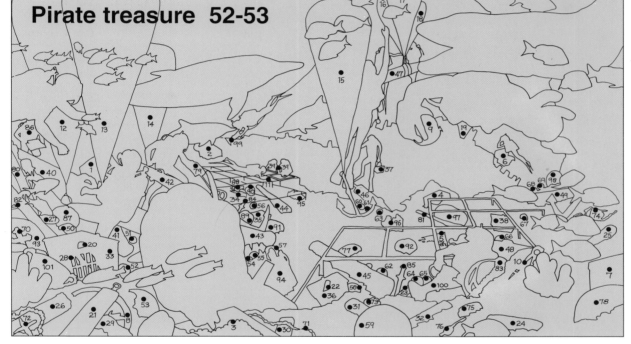

Pirate treasure 52-53

Chests of coins 1 2 3 4 5 6 7
Astrolabe 8
Sundial 9
Dividers 10
Camera 11
Lifting bags 12 13 14 15 16 17 18 19
Gold ingots 20 21 22 23 24 25
Silver ingots 26 27 28 29 30 31 32
Baskets 33 34 35 36 37 38
Divers measuring 39
Cannons 40 41 42 43 44 45 46 47 48 49
Cannonballs 50 51 52 53 54 55 56 57 58 59 60 61 62 63 64 65 66 67 68 69
Emerald cross 70
Gold chain 71
Rosary 72
Emerald ring 73
Gold locket 74
Buckle 75
Whistle 76
Gold plates 77 78

Metal detector 79
Muskets 80 81
Swords 82 83
Daggers 84 85
Diver sketching 86
Jars 87 88 89 90 91 92
Barrels 93 94 95 96 97 98
Hand blowers 99 100
Gold cup 101

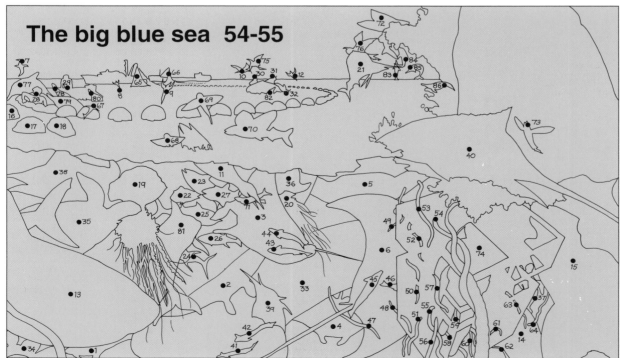

The big blue sea 54-55

Manta rays 1 2 3 4 5 6
Boobies 7 8 9 10 11 12
Great white sharks 13 14 15
Portuguese men-of-war 16 17 18 19 20
Sailfish 21
Yellow fin tuna 22 23 24 25 26 27
Fishermen 28 29 30 31 32
Whale shark 33
Leatherback turtles 34 35 36 37
Marlins 38 39 40
Remoras 41 42 43 44 45 46
Sea snakes 47 48 49 50 51 52 53 54 55 56 57 58 59 60 61 62 63 64
Purse seine nets 65 66
Flying fish 67 68 69 70 71 72 73
Diver in cage 74
Frigate birds 75 76

Spinner dolphins 77 78 79 80 81 82 83 84 85 86

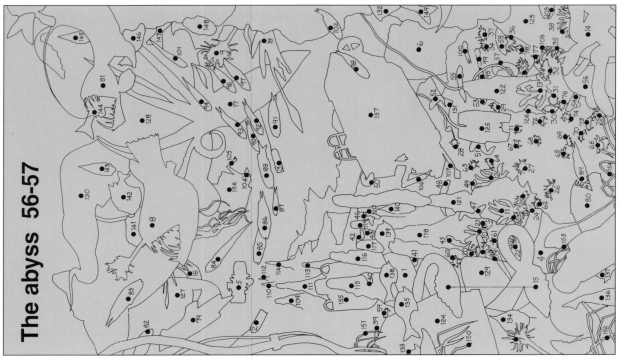

The abyss 56-57

Sonar "fish" 1 2 3
Tripod fish 4
Bathyscaphes 5 6
Angler fish 7 8 9
Beardworms 10 11 12 13 14
Giant squid 15 16 17 18
Anemones 19 20 21 22 23 24 25 26 27 28 29 30 31 32 33 34 35 36 37 38
Vent fish 39 40 41 42 43 44 45 46 47 48 49 50 51 52 53 54 55 56 57 58
Crabs 59 60 61 62 63 64 65 66 67 68 69 70 71 72 73 74 75 76 77 78
Deep Flight 79
Viper fish 80 81
Lantern fish 82 83 84 85 86 87 88 89 90 91 92 93 94 95 96 97 98 99 100 101 102 103

Manipulator arms 104 105 106 107 108
Black smokers 109 110 111 112 113 114 115 116 117 118 119 120 121 122 123
ROVs 124 125 126
Sperm whales 127 128
Gulper eels 129 130 131 132
Hatchet fish 133 134 135 136 137 138 139 140 141 142 143 144 145 146 147 148 149
Deep sea spiders 150 151 152 153 154
Submersibles:
  Turtle 155
  Alvin 156
  Nautile 157

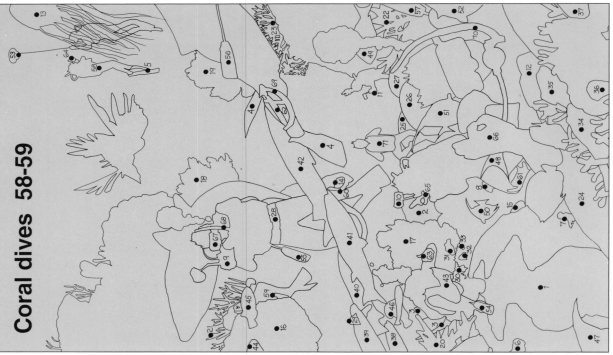

Coral dives 58-59

Giant clams 1 2
Yellow fins 3 4 5
Sea slugs 6 7 8
Cameras 9 10 11 12
Sea wasp 13
Olive sea snake 14
Cone shell 15
Coral:
  Sea fan 16 17 18 19
  Staghorn 20 21 22 23
  Brain 24 25 26 27
Diver with six weights 28
Clown fish 29 30 31 32 33 34 35 36 37
Barracudas 38 39 40 41 42
Pink BC 43
Clown triggerfish 44 45 46
Surgeon fish 47 48 49
Moorish idol 50 51 52
Marker buoy 53
Consoles 54 55 56 57

Diver in short pink wetsuit 58
Knives 59 60 61 62
Divers' signals:
  "Let's go up" 63 64
  "I'm OK" 65 66
Leaking mask 67
Blue snorkels 68 69 70
Diver with two tanks 71

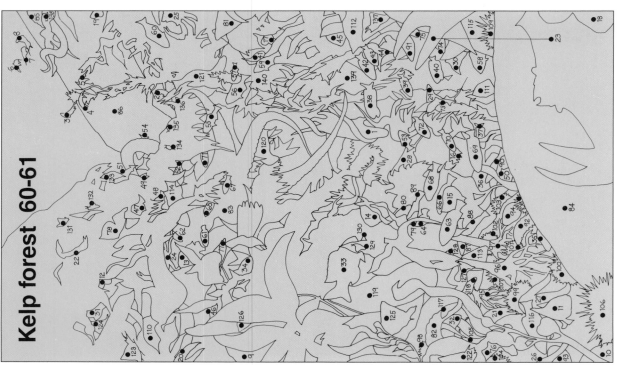

Kelp forest 60-61

Sea otters 1 2 3 4 5 6 7 8
Ocean goldfish 9 10 11 12 13 14 15 16 17 18 19
Kelp crabs 20 21 22 23 24 25
Sea stars 26 27
Bat rays 28 29 30
Blacksmiths 31 32 33 34 35 36 37 38 39 40 41 42 43 44 45
Halfmoons 46 47 48 49 50 51 52 53 54 55 56 57 58 59 60
Opaleyes 61 62 63 64 65 66 67 68 69 70 71 72 73 74 75
Giant kelpfish 76 77 78 79 80 81
Giant octopuses 82 83 84 85
Ship 86
Senoritas 87 88 89 90 91
Abalone 92
Empty abalone shells 93 94
Holdfasts 95 96 97

Red sea urchins 98 99 100 101 102 103
Purple sea urchins 104 105 106 107 108 109
Sheephead wrasses:
  male 110 111 112
  female 113 114 115
  young 116 117 118
Sealions 119 120 121
Sea snails 122 123 124 125 126 127 128 129 130 131 132 133 134 135 136 137 138
Gray whales:
  mother 139
  baby 140

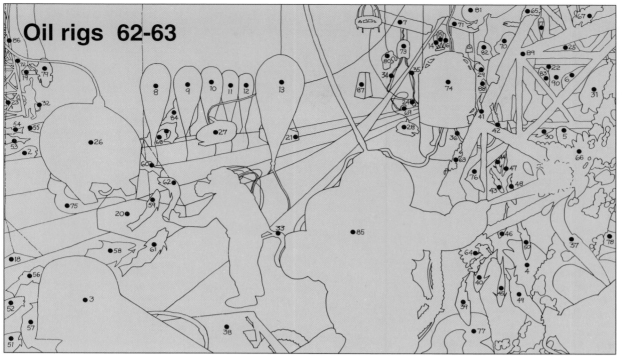

Oil rigs 62-63

Helmet with square face plate 1
Seals 2 3 4 5 6
Diving support vessel 7
Airbags 8 9 10 11 12 13 14 15 16 17
Tool baskets 18 19 20 21 22
Work ROVs 23 24 25
Eyeball ROVs 26 27 28 29 30 31
Umbilicals 32 33 34 35 36 37
Water jet pump 38
Pollack 39 40 41 42 43 44 45 46 47 48 49 50
Cod 51 52 53 54 55 56 57 58 59 60 61 62
Mussels 63 64 65 66 67
Divers cutting 68 69 70
Pipe-laying barge 71
Diving bells 72 73 74
Conger eels 75 76 77 78
Wasp suits 79 80 81 82 83
Newtsuits 84 85
Rigs 86 87 88 89 90

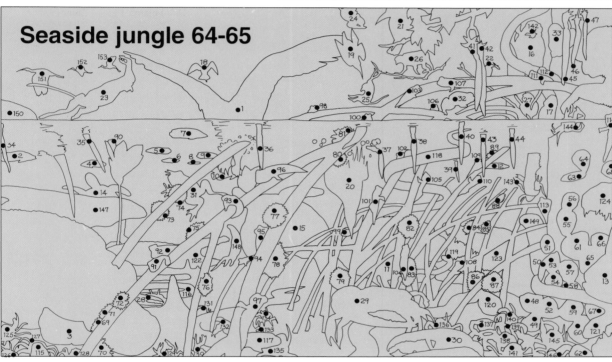

Seaside jungle 64-65

Osprey 1
Tripletail fish 2 3 4 5 6 7 8 9 10 11 12 13
Turtles 14 15
Crab-eating macaques 16 17
Kingfishers 18 19 20 21 22
Proboscis monkeys 23 24 25 26 27
Male fiddler crabs 28 29 30
Crab-eating frogs 31 32 33
Mangrove seedlings 34 35 36 37 38 39 40 41 42 43 44 45 46 47
Oysters 48 49 50 51 52 53 54 55 56 57 58 59 60 61 62 63 64 65 66 67 68
Chama 69 70 71 72 73 74 75 76 77 78 79 80 81 82 83 84 85 86 87 88 89
Mudskippers 90 91 92 93 94 95 96 97 98 99 100
101 102 103 104 105 106 107 108 109 110 111 112 113 114
Dog-headed sea snakes 115 116 117 118 119 120 121
Saltwater crocodiles 122 123 124
Soldier crabs 125 126 127 128 129 130 131 132 133 134 135 136 137 138 139 140 141 142 143 144 145 146
Otters 147 148 149
Glossy ibis 150 151 152 153

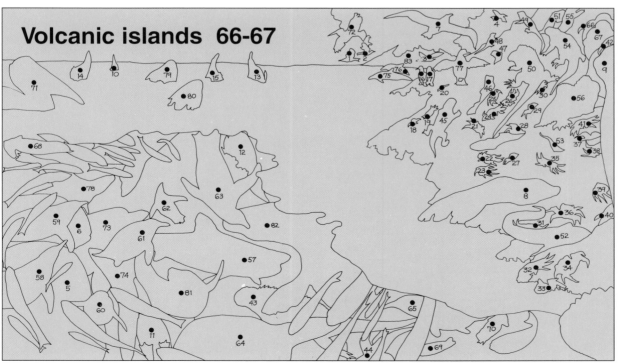

Volcanic islands 66-67

Swallow-tailed gulls 1 2 3 4
Pilot whale:
  adult 5
  baby 6
Albatross 7
Fur seals 8 9
Red-footed boobies 10 11 12 13
Blue-footed boobies 14 15 16 17
Sally lightfoot crabs 18 19 20 21 22 23 24 25 26 27 28 28 30 31 32 33 34 35 36 37 38 39 40 41 42
Marine iguanas 43 44 45 46 47 48 49 50 51 52 53 54 55 56
Tiger shark 57
Penguins 58 59 60 61 62 63 64 65
Male frigate birds 66 67
Squid 68 69 70
Pelicans 71 72
Spotted dolphins 73 74
Common dolphins 75 76
Cormorant 77
Sealions 78 79 80 81 82
Volcanic island erupting 83

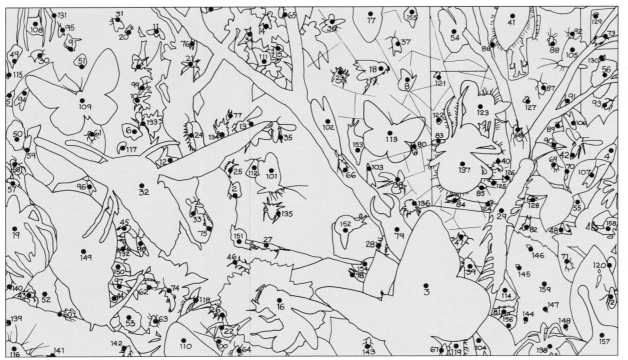

Homes and gardens 70-71

Male common blue butterflies 1 2 3 4
Female common blue butterflies 5 6 7 8
Honeybees 9 10 11 12 13 14 15 16 17 18
Zebra spiders 19 20 21 22 23
Centipedes 24 25 26 27 28 29
Wasps 30 31 32 33 34 35 36 37 38 39 40 41 42
Devil's coach-horses 43 44 45 46 47 48
Spittle bugs 49 50 51 52 53 54 55 56
Greenflies 57 58 59 60 61 62 63 64 65 66 67 68 69 70 71 72 73
Earwigs 74 75 76 77 78 79 80 81 82

Cockroaches 83 84 85 86 87 88 89 90 91 92 93
Lacewings 94 95 96 97 98 99 100 101 102 103 104 105 106 107
Cinnabar moths 108 109 110 111 112 113 114
Cinnabar moth caterpillars 115 116 117 118 119 120
Houseflies 121 122 123 124 125 126 127 128 129 130
Garden spiders 131 132 133 134 135 136 137 138
Fleas 139 140 141 142 143 144 145 146 147 148
Snails 149 150 151 152 153 154 155 156 157 158
Cat 159

Cactus city 72-73

Tarantula hawk wasps 1 2 3 4 5 6 7
Trapdoor spiders 8 9 10 11
Scorpions 12 13 14 15 16 17
Giant red velvet mites 18 19 20 21 22 23 24 25 26 27
Honey ants 28 29 30 31 32 33 34 35 36 37 38 39 40
Blister beetles 41 42 43 44
Black widow spiders 45 46 47 48
Tarantulas 49 50 51 52 53 54
Yucca moths 55 56 57 58 59
Lynx spiders 60 61 62 63 64
Ant-lion larvae 65 66 67
Whip scorpions 68 69 70 71 72

Hercules beetles 73 74 75 76 77 78
Harvester ants 79 80 81 82 83 84 85 86 87 88 89 90 91 92 93
Painted grasshoppers 94 95 96 97 98 99 100 101 102 103
Red-kneed bird-eating spiders 104 105 106 107
Burrowing owl 108

Island paradise 74-75

Praying mantis nymphs 1 2 3 4
Lynx spiders 5 6 7 8
Pill millipedes 9 10 11 12 13 14
Rosea bugs 15 16 17 18 19 20 21 22 23 24 25 26 27 28 29 30 31 32 33 34 35 36 37 38 39 40 41
Yellow hairy weevils 42 43 44 45 46 47 48
Brown hairy weevils 49 50 51 52 53 54 55
Longhorn beetles 56 57 58 59 60 61 62
Butterflies with open wings 63 64 65 66 67 68
Butterflies with shut wings 69 70 71 72 73
Shield bug adults 74 75 76 77

Shield bug nymphs 78 79 80 81
Hissing cockroaches 82 83 84 85 86
Giant millipedes 87 88 89 90 91
Thorn spiders 92 93 94 95
Stick insects 96 97 98
Emperor dragonflies 99 100 101 102 103 104
Giraffe-necked weevils 105 106 107 108
Flatworms 109 110 111 112
Red dragonflies 113 114 115 116
Ring-tailed lemur 117
Blue tree boa 118

Dazzling display 76-77

Leaf beetles
1 2 3 4 5 6 7 8 9
Wandering
spiders 10 11
Thornbugs
12 13 14 15 16
17 18 19 20 21
Hamadryas
butterflies
22 23 24 25
Stilt bugs
26 27 28 29 30
Bright bugs 31
32 33 34 35 36
Harlequin
beetles 37 38 39
40 41 42 43
Grasshoppers
44 45 46
Bark bugs 47 48
49 50 51 52 53
Leafcutter ants
54 55 56 57 58
59 60 61 62 63
64 65 66 67 68
69
Hercules beetles
70 71 72 73
Morpho
butterflies
74 75 76 77

Black and yellow
grasshoppers
78 79 80
Yellow, black and
red grasshoppers
81 82 83
Hawk moth
caterpillars
84 85 86 87 88
Assassin bugs
89 90 91 92 93
94 95
Tapir 96

Between the trees 78-79

Net throwing
spiders 1 2 3
Crickets
4 5 6 7 8
Bogong moths
9 10 11 12
Common grass
yellow butterflies
13 14 15 16 17
18 19 20 21 22
23 24 25 26 27
28 29 30 31 32
33 34 35
Emperor gum
moth caterpillars
36 37 38 39
Gliding spiders
40 41 42 43
Monarch
butterflies
44 45 46 47 48
Shield bugs
49 50 51 52 53
54 55 56 57
Witchetty grubs
58 59 60 61 62
63
Giant stick
insects
64 65 66 67

Bulldog ants
68 69 70 71 72
73 74 75 76 77
78 79
Sydney funnel-
web spiders
80 81 82 83
Processionary
moth caterpillars
84 85 86 87 88
89 90 91 92 93
94
Redback spiders
95 96 97
Sawfly larvae 98
99 100 101 102
103 104 105 106
Emperor gum
moths
107 108 109
Bandicoot 110

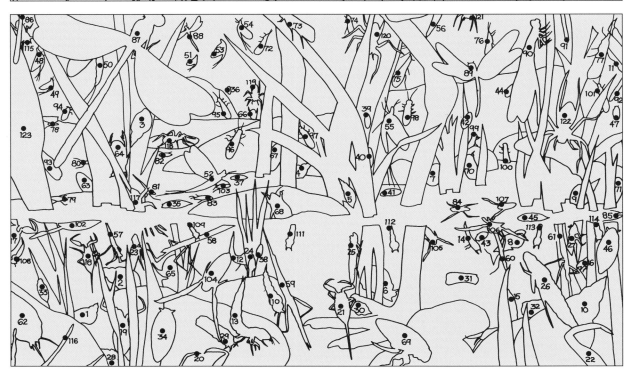

Water world 80-81

Pond snails
1 2 3 4 5 6
7 8 9 10 11
Great diving
beetle larvae
12 13 14 15 16
Water scorpions
17 18 19 20 21
22
Dragonfly
nymphs
23 24 25 26 27
Caddisfly larvae
28 29 30 31 32
Whirligig beetles
33 34 35 36 37
38 39 40 41 42
43 44 45 46 47
Mayflies
48 49 50 51 52
53 54 55 56
Water stick
insects
57 58 59 60 61
Great diving
beetles
62 63 64 65 66
67 68 69 70 71
Caddisflies
72 73 74 75 76
77

Water striders
78 79 80 81 82
83 84 85
Damselflies
86 87 88 89 90
91 92
Stoneflies
93 94 95 96 97
98 99 100 101
Backswimmers
102 103 104 105
106 107
Mosquito larvae
108 109 110 111
112 113 114
Fisher spiders
115 116 117 118
119 120 121 122
Great white
heron 123

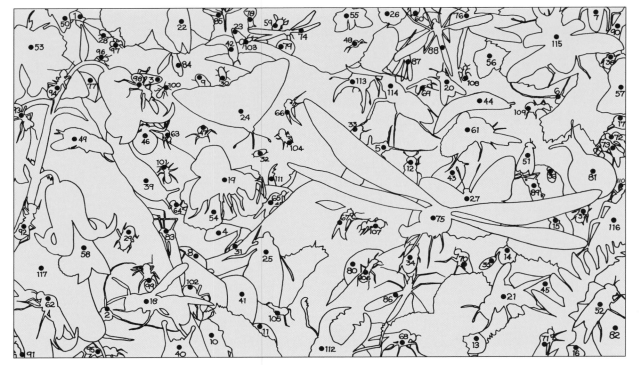

In the woods 82-83

Longhorn beetles	72 73
1 2 3 4 5 6 7	Darter dragonflies
Burying beetles	74 75 76
8 9 10 11 12 13	Hedge snails
14 15 16 17	77 78 79 80 81
Hornets	82
18 19 20 21	Crane flies
Purple emperor butterflies	83 84 85 86 87
22 23 24 25 26	88 89 90
27	Wood ants
Bark beetles	91 92 93 94 95
28 29 30 31 32	96 97 98 99 100
33 34 35 36 37	101 102 103 104
38	105 106 107 108
Slugs	109 110
39 40 41 42 43	Stag beetles
44 45	111 112 113 114
Crab spiders	115 116
46 47 48	Hedgehog 117
Horseflies	
49 50 51 52	
Poplar hawk moths	
53 54 55 56 57	
Bumblebees	
58 59 60 61	
Empid flies	
62 63 64 65 66	
67 68 69 70 71	

Swamp life 84-85

Tree snails	Fiddler crabs
1 2 3 4 5 6 7 8 9	76 77 78 79 80
10 11 12	81
Viceroy butterflies	Io moths
13 14 15 16 17	82 83 84 85 86
Blue land crabs	Apple snails
18 19 20 21 22	87 88 89 90 91
23 24 25 26 27	92
28 29 30 31	Apple snail eggs
Green darner dragonflies	93 94 95
32 33 34 35 36	Golden orb weaver spiders
Lubber grasshoppers	96 97 98
37 38 39 40	Alligator 99
Fisher spiders	
41 42 43	
Zebra butterflies	
44 45 46 47	
Midge larvae	
48 49 50 51 52	
53 54	
Giant water bugs	
55 56 57 58	
Jumping spiders	
59 60 61	
Mosquitoes	
62 63 64 65 66	
67 68 69 70 71	
72 73 74 75	

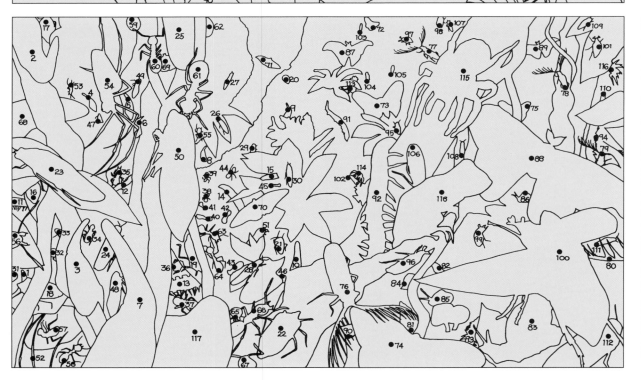

Deep in the jungle 86-87

Lantern bugs	Yellow snails
1 2 3 4 5 6	81 82 83
7 8 9 10	Brown snails
Flat-backed millipedes	84 85 86
11 12 13 14 15	Atlas moths
Shield bugs	87 88 89
16 17 18 19 20	Red centipedes
21 22	90 91 92 93 94
Jewel beetles	Cockchafer beetles
23 24 25 26 27	95 96 97 98 99
28 29 30	100 101
Termites	Fireflies
31 32 33 34 35	102 103 104 105
36 37 38 39 40	106 107 108 109
41 42 43 44 45	110 111 112
46	Hairy bird-eating spiders
Cicadas	113 114 115 116
47 48 49 50 51	Orangutan 117
Nephila spiders	Green tree frog
52 53 54 55	118
Weaver ants	
56 57 58 59 60	
61 62 63 64 65	
66 67	
Birdwing butterflies	
68 69 70 71	
Loepa moths	
72 73 74 75	
Longicorn beetles	
76 77 78 79 80	

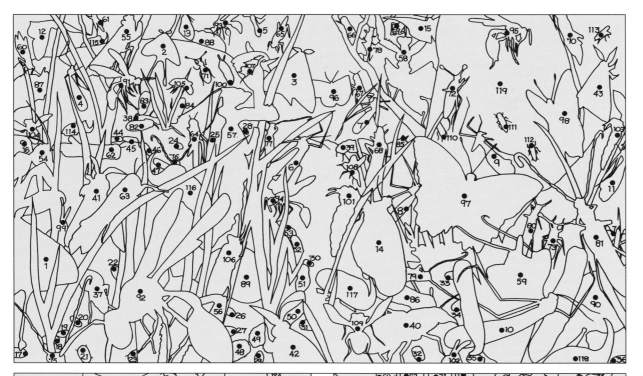
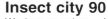

Minibeast safari 88-89

African moon moths
1 2 3
Hanging flies
4 5 6 7 8 9 10 11
Monarch butterflies
12 13 14 15
Histerid beetles
16 17 18 19 20
21 22 23 24 25
26 27 28 29 30
31 32 33 34 35
36
Ground beetles
37 38 39 40
Processionary moths
41 42 43
Processionary moth caterpillars
44 45 46 47 48
49 50 51 52 53
Praying mantids
54 55 56 57 58
59
Locusts 60 61
62 63 64 65 66
67 68 69 70
Stalk-eyed flies
71 72 73 74

Longhorn beetles
75 76 77 78 79
80 81
African assassin bugs
82 83 84 85 86
African land snails
87 88 89 90
Potter wasps
91 92 93 94 95
Swallowtail butterflies
96 97 98
Swallowtail butterfly caterpillars
99 100 101 102 103
Tsetse flies
104 105 106 107
108 109 110 111
112 113
Rhinoceros beetles
114 115 116 117 118
Kudu 119

Insect city 90

Workers carrying leaves
78 79 80 81 82 83 84
Soldier termites
85 86 87 88 89 90 91 92 93 94 95 96 97 98 99 100 101 102 103 104

Larvae 105 106
107 108 109 110
111 112 113 114
115 116 117 118
119 120 121 122
123 124 125 126
127
Nurseries
128 129 130 131
King termite 132
Queen termite 133
Aardvark 134

Busy beehive 91

Queen bee 1
Drones 2 3 4 5 6 7 8
Workers huddling around the queen 9 10 11
Workers carrying balls of pollen 12 13 14
Workers feeding larvae 15 16 17
Worker spitting 18
Pollen cells
19 20 21 22 23
24 25 26 27 28

Egg cells 29 30
31 32 33 34 35
36 37 38 39 40
Larvae cells
41 42 43 44 45
46 47 48 49 50
51 52 53 54 55
56 57
Honey cells
58 59 60 61 62
63 64 65 66 67
68 69 70 71
Fungus gardens
72 73 74 75 76 77
Mouse 135

Little Bug Puzzle

1. Which of these bugs lives only in Madagascar?
a) Zebra butterflies
b) Whirligig beetle
c) Hairy weevils
d) Giant red velvet mites

2. Which of these bugs is not yellow?
a) Loepa moths
b) Longhorn beetles
c) Flatworms
d) Bogong moths

3. How many different kinds of spiders are there in *The Big Bug Search?*

4. Which of these have tummies which light up, then flash on and off?
a) Lantern bugs
b) Fireflies
c) Bright bugs
d) Jewel beetles

5. Which of these could be found in the eucalyptus forests of eastern Australia or on safari in Africa?
a) Redback spiders
b) Emperor gum moths
c) Monarch butterflies
d) Rhinoceros beetles

6. How many eggs can a queen termite lay in one day?

Answers on page 111

107

Index

Answers

Answers to Little Bug Puzzle on page 107: 1. c) 2. d) 3. 18 spiders 4. b) 5. c)
6. She can lay over 30,000 eggs a day.